PUFFIN BOOKS

mermaid curse

The Golden Circlet

Born in Hertfordshire, England, on 29 May 1952, Louise Cooper describes herself as 'a typical scatterbrained Gemini'. She spent most of her school years writing stories when she should have been concentrating on lessons, and her first fantasy novel, *The Book of Paradox*, was published in 1973, when she was just twenty years old. Since then she has published more than eighty books for adults and children.

Louise now lives in Cornwall with her husband, Cas Sandall. When she isn't writing, she enjoys singing (and playing various instruments), cooking, gardening, 'messing about on the beach' and – just to make sure she keeps busy – is also treasurer of her local Royal National Lifeboat Institution branch.

Visit Louise at her own website at louisecooper.com

Books by Louise Cooper

Sea Horses series in reading order

Sea Horses
The Talisman
Gathering Storm
The Last Secret

Mermaid Curse series in reading order

The Silver Dolphin
The Black Pearl
The Rainbow Pool
The Golden Circlet

Mermaid Curse

The Golden Circlet

LOUISE COOPER

PUFFIN

PUFFIN BOOKS

Published by the Penguin Group
Penguin Books Ltd, 80 Strand, London WC2R ORL, England
Penguin Group (USA) Inc., 375 Hudson Street, New York, New York 10014, USA
Penguin Group (Canada), 90 Eglinton Avenue East, Suite 700, Toronto, Ontario, Canada M4P 2Y3
(a division of Pearson Penguin Canada Inc.)
Penguin Ireland, 25 St Stephen's Green, Dublin 2, Ireland (a division of Penguin Books Ltd)
Penguin Group (Australia), 250 Camberwell Road, Camberwell, Victoria 3124, Australia
(a division of Pearson Australia Group Pty Ltd)
Penguin Books India Pvt Ltd, 11 Community Centre, Panchsheel Park, New Delhi – 110 017, India
Penguin Group (NZ), 67 Apollo Drive, Rosedale, North Shore 0632, New Zealand
(a division of Pearson New Zealand Ltd)
Penguin Books (South Africa) (Pty) Ltd, 24 Sturdee Avenue, Rosebank,
Johannesburg 2196, South Africa

Penguin Books Ltd, Registered Offices: 80 Strand, London WC2R ORL, England

puffinbooks.com

First published 2008
1

Text copyright © Louise Cooper, 2008
All rights reserved

The moral right of the author has been asserted

Set in Sabon by Palimpsest Book Production Ltd, Grangemouth, Stirlingshire
Made and printed in England by Clays Ltd, St Ives plc

British Library Cataloguing in Publication Data
A CIP catalogue record for this book is available from the British Library

ISBN: 978-0-141-32228-5

For Marina and Clemency Scott,
who first dived into my mystical adventures
at Pendennis Castle

Prologue

Rose stared at her younger sister, Lizzy. 'I shouldn't believe a word of what you've told me,' she said in a quiet voice. 'It's totally nuts, totally insane, and I shouldn't believe it. But I saw it with my own eyes. The mermaid with hair just like yours. And Kes – only he wasn't an ordinary boy any more; he had a fish's tail. And you were swimming in the sea with them, just as if you were a mermaid too.' She blinked, and shook her head vigorously as if to clear it. 'That is . . . I suppose you *are* a mermaid, aren't you?'

Lizzy hesitated for a moment, then slowly nodded. 'Yes,' she said. 'I didn't believe it at first, either. I felt just the same as you. But it's true, Rose. The mermaid you saw – Morvyr – is my real mother.'

'And Kes is –'

'My twin brother. But he grew up under the sea, so he learned a lot of things that I don't know. Like how to change his shape between human and merboy.'

'Can *you* do that too?' Rose asked wonderingly.

Lizzy gave an odd little laugh. 'I can breathe underwater – the dolphins taught me that when I first found out the truth. And Kes says I *can* change my shape. But I've tried and tried, and I can't make it work.'

Rose was silent as she tried to come to terms with what she had learned. She and Lizzy had been told years ago that they were both adopted, but though Rose knew about her own parents, Lizzy had been found abandoned when she was a baby and her past had always been a mystery. The knowledge that her sister was only half human was the strangest thing that had ever happened to

Rose. She had stopped believing in mermaids long ago. Now, though . . .

Lizzy, too, said nothing. She knew how Rose must be feeling, for she had felt the same herself when this adventure began. It was a story beyond her wildest imagination. And it had all happened in just a few short weeks, since the girls and their adoptive parents had moved to Cornwall, and Lizzy met a boy called Kes on the beach. Kes had recognized her as his long-lost twin sister. And he had told her the astounding truth about her real family.

Years ago, a shipwrecked fisherman named Jack Carrick had been rescued by the mermaid Morvyr, and they fell in love. Kara, the mermaid Queen, cast a spell that enabled Jack to live under the sea; he and Morvyr were married, and twin babies – Lizzy and Kes – were born to them. But the family's happiness was short-lived, for soon afterwards Queen Kara had been attacked and killed by the evil Taran. Taran usurped the throne and stole the golden crown with its nine magical pearls that were the source of the Queen's power. But before she died Kara had taken two of the pearls – one black and one silver – and given them to Morvyr, begging her to keep them safe.

Taran wanted those pearls at any cost, for without them her power was incomplete. She had tried to force Morvyr to tell her where they were and, when she failed, she kidnapped Lizzy in revenge and abandoned her on the shore just a few miles from Morvyr's undersea home.

Tricked into thinking she had been taken far away, Lizzy's human father, Jack, travelled the world for eleven years, searching for her. For eleven years, too, Taran hunted vainly for the black and silver pearls. But now Jack had come home. Morvyr had given him the black pearl for safe-keeping. And the silver pearl was in a secret compartment in the locket that Lizzy had been wearing when she was abandoned.

Or it had been – until Taran found out the truth and had forced the twins to give her the silver pearl. Now only the black pearl stood between her and the power she craved.

And only Lizzy and her new-found family could stop her from getting it.

Lizzy spoke at last. 'It's got to be our secret, Rose. Ours and my – my other family's. You mustn't tell a living soul about it.'

Rose gave her a long look, then smiled. 'Course I won't,' she said. 'Anyway, who would ever believe me? People don't think that mermaids and magic and things like that are real.'

'But they are,' said Lizzy softly. 'We both know they are.'

There was silence again for some moments. Then Rose reached out and took hold of Lizzy's hand. 'Yes,' she said. 'We do, don't we?'

Chapter One

'Well, I must say it makes a nice change to be going out as a family,' said Mr Baxter as he locked the car door and followed the others towards the car park entrance. 'We ought to do it more often.'

'I can't wait to see the prize exhibit,' said Mrs Baxter. 'I'd love to have been at the harbour when it was brought in!' She looked at her two daughters. 'You girls certainly caused a stir there, didn't you?'

Lizzy and Rose exchanged a glance, and Lizzy said, 'It wasn't really anything to do with us, Mum. Mr Treleaven and Ja– I mean, Mr Carrick did it all. We were just lucky, being there when it happened.'

Rose raised eyebrows at her and silently mouthed something that Lizzy thought was, *Oh, yeah, and the rest!* Lizzy ignored it, though she could feel her cheeks turning pink.

They crossed the road and followed the signs to the Sealife Centre. The town was crowded with August holidaymakers, and Rose wanted to stop and look in all the shops selling surf wear and jewellery and accessories, but the others hurried her on. The Centre was a long building overlooking one of the town's beaches and reached by a flight of steps. There was a queue to get in, but it wasn't a long one; in this glorious weather most people wanted to be on the sand rather than indoors. As they waited their turn, Lizzy looked across the beach to the sea in the distance. White surf was creaming and pounding at the low tideline, and the sound of it was a ceaseless background roar. This north coast of Cornwall was very different, she thought, from

the south side where they lived. Instead of
harbours and quiet inlets, there were endless
stretches of smooth, golden sand, with cliffs rising
like huge buttresses behind them, dark against the
blue sky. The beach was dotted with the bright
colours of towels and rugs and windbreaks as
more and more holidaymakers arrived to spread
themselves out on the sand, and in the distance
Lizzy could see the lifeguards in their familiar red-
and-yellow clothing patrolling near the sea's edge.

The Baxters reached the head of the queue,
paid their entrance fee and went into the
aquarium. As they moved from brightness to the
dimly lit interior, Lizzy's heart gave a nervous little
skip. The 'prize exhibit' that Mum was so eager to
look at had been caught at sea by the fishing
trawler *Regard*, owned by Mr Treleaven, the
father of Rose's boyfriend, Paul. Lizzy and Rose
had been on board the boat, and they knew that
there was far, far more to the story than Mum
and Dad could ever imagine. For on that eventful
trip Rose had learned Lizzy's incredible secret –

and had witnessed the latest attempt by Taran, the evil mermaid Queen, to get her hands on the precious black pearl.

It had been a terrifying experience for both the girls. But Taran's bid had failed when her servant, a monstrous conger eel, tried to attack the *Regard* and was caught in the trawl net. The eel now had a new home. And that was why Lizzy and Rose were here.

The dark-walled corridor wound through the aquarium, with lit tanks on both sides. The tanks held a wonderful array of sea creatures: brightly coloured fish, scurrying crabs, beautiful corals and anemones, and one big, cylindrical tank where sea horses hovered and drifted among a forest of slender, living seaweeds. Mr and Mrs Baxter kept pausing to look at the displays, but Rose and Lizzy found it hard to concentrate. They were both impatient to see just one creature.

'Mum and Dad are miles behind,' Rose said after a while, looking back. 'We'd better wait for them to catch up.'

They stopped beside a tank where a single incredibly ugly fish peered out at them from between two rocks. Rose stared at it, but she was thinking of something else. 'What did you say that eel was called?' she whispered.

'Tullor,' Lizzy whispered back, and suppressed a shiver. Just Tullor's name was enough to bring back unpleasant memories.

'I can't believe he's really as big as he looked out at sea.'

'Oh, he is,' said Lizzy with feeling. 'But don't forget that he's – he *was* – Queen Taran's top henchman. He was probably an ordinary eel to start with, but she could have used her magical powers to change him.'

'You mean, she made him bigger, and more intelligent . . . things like that?'

'I don't know for sure, but I wouldn't be surprised.'

'Mmm.' Then Rose smiled. 'She must be absolutely livid about losing him.'

This time Lizzy couldn't stop the shiver from

showing. 'Oh, shut up! I don't want to even *think* about Taran! Facing Tullor's going to be bad enough.'

Rose was surprised. 'If that's how you feel, why did you want to come and see him?'

'I don't know, really. I suppose . . .' Lizzy hesitated, then shrugged. 'I suppose I wanted to make sure that he really *is* here and can't cause any more trouble. I still have bad dreams about him −' She broke off. 'Shh, here come Mum and Dad.'

They all moved on together. Mrs Baxter was enchanted by the sea horses, and was still talking about them as they rounded the next bend in the corridor. Then suddenly Lizzy stopped, staring.

Ahead of them, a small crowd of people was gathered in front of a wall of solid glass; a tank far bigger than anything they had yet seen. The light inside it was dim, and there was an artificial rock face at the back, stretching from floor to ceiling. Nothing else was visible in the gloom, but Lizzy's heart started to thump. Something was in there. She could feel its presence. And she knew what it was.

'Aha!' Dad's voice broke the spell that had gripped her. 'This looks promising.' He squeezed in between two goggling people and read the notice on the wall beside the tank. 'Yes, he's in here. "The biggest conger eel ever recorded in Cornwall"!'

Mum joined him and they stood among the spectators and peered into the tank's depths, trying to get a glimpse of its occupant. Rose went to look too, but Lizzy hung back. She wanted – *needed* – to know that Tullor was safely imprisoned in the tank. But she dreaded actually seeing him. Worse still, she dreaded the thought of him seeing her.

'There he is!' said Dad eagerly, pointing. 'See his head, poking out from that crevice in the rock?'

'Oh, yes!' cried Mum. 'Wow, he really *is* a giant, isn't he?' She looked over her shoulder. 'Come on, Lizzy, come and have a look.'

Lizzy had a sudden attack of nerves. She wanted to say that she didn't want to push in, but to her dismay people moved aside to make room for her. Heart pounding harder than ever, she approached the tank. At first she could see only the rock wall. But then something moved slightly, and with a shock she realized that she was gazing straight into the cold, cruel and alien eyes of a huge conger eel. For a few moments she and Tullor stared at each other. Then, very slowly, the eel opened his mouth, revealing rows of incurved, razor-sharp teeth. It was as if he was silently snarling . . . and the snarl was for her alone. He had recognized her, and she felt the sheer power of his hatred radiating towards her like the heat of a fire.

The other people moved on, exclaiming to each other about Tullor's size, and Dad let his breath out in a whistle. 'Whoo, what a brute! I'm amazed he didn't sink the boat when you caught him!'

'Mr Treleaven's a brilliant fisherman,' said Rose. She, too, was staring at Tullor, and there was a slight frown on her face.

'He'd have to be, to land a creature like that!' Dad's voice was full of admiration. 'Well, all I can say is, well done all of you!'

Mum was studying the details on the printed notice. 'I wonder what they feed him on?' she mused. 'It doesn't say.'

'He looks as if he'd eat just about anything,' said Dad. 'Including sharks, whales and a few swimmers, if they don't watch out!'

'That's it.' Mum grinned. 'He's the British Jaws!'

They both laughed. But Lizzy didn't join in. Tullor was still glaring at her, and though her first rush of fear had worn off, that cold, unwavering stare made her feel very uncomfortable. With an effort she dragged her gaze away and said, 'Well, we've seen him now, and he doesn't look as if he's going to come out. Shall we move on?'

Mum and Dad agreed. The three of them started to walk away and were about to turn the corner of the passage when Lizzy realized that Rose had not followed them. She looked back, and saw her sister still standing in front of the tank. Rose was frowning, as though trying to work something out. And Tullor was staring at her.

'Come on, Rose.' Lizzy tried to sound casual, but she felt uneasy.

Rose didn't answer. In fact, she didn't seem to have heard. For a few more seconds she looked back at Tullor, not moving, not even blinking. Then, slowly, Tullor's gaping mouth closed, and his head withdrew into the crevice until he was out of sight.

Rose shook her head like someone coming out of a daydream. Then suddenly she swayed violently.

'Rose!' Lizzy cried in alarm. 'What's up?'

Mum heard and turned round, in time to see Rose cover her face with both hands as she staggered backwards and collided with Lizzy.

'Rose, whatever's the matter?' Mum and Dad both hurried to her, and Mum caught hold of her as it seemed she was about to collapse to the floor.

'Ohh . . . I feel so *dizzy* . . .' Rose mumbled.

'Come on, love, it's all right,' Mum soothed. 'Do you want to sit down somewhere?'

'N-no, it . . . it's going away now.' Rose swallowed and shook her head again. 'I'm OK, honestly.'

'It's probably the peculiar light in here,' said Dad. 'And it's very warm too. Best get her into the open. There's a cafe upstairs, with an outside balcony. Something to drink will help her feel better.'

Rose was unsteady as Mr and Mrs Baxter led her towards the nearest exit. Lizzy followed, worried. *Was* it just the heat and the strange lighting that had made Rose giddy? It seemed like a reasonable explanation, but Lizzy had her doubts. She couldn't imagine how, but she had a sneaking feeling that Tullor might have had something to do with it.

In the cafe Rose quickly recovered, helped by a flapjack and a banana milkshake. She told Mum to stop fussing, and within minutes was back to her usual cheerful and slightly bossy self. No, she said, she didn't want to go into the aquarium again; on a day like this it would be more fun to go on the beach and watch the surfers. If Mum and Dad wanted to see the rest of the exhibits, fine; she'd meet them somewhere later.

'Well, I suppose you could,' said Mum dubiously. 'And I *would* like to finish going through; there are lots of things we haven't seen yet. But I don't like the thought of you going off on your own, in case you feel ill again.'

'I'll go with her, Mum,' Lizzy said quickly. 'I'm not bothered about the aquarium. And I've got my mobile, so if there's a problem I can ring you.'

'Well . . . all right, then. Meet us back here in an hour.'

Rose finished her milkshake and she and Lizzy left the building and went down the steps that led to the beach. As they walked along the sand towards the distant tideline Rose asked, 'Didn't you want to see the rest of the aquarium?'

'Not really,' said Lizzy. 'Like I said, I just wanted

to know that Tullor really is safely out of the way.'

'Mmm.' Rose narrowed her eyes as she stared at the sea. Then, thoughtfully, she added, 'I'm glad he wasn't killed, though. I know he is evil, but I feel sort of . . . sorry for him.'

Lizzy was astonished. '*Sorry?*' she echoed.

'In a way.' Rose sounded defensive. 'I mean, it couldn't have been a bag of laughs being a servant to that Queen creature. If what you've told me about her is true –'

'It *is* true!'

'OK, OK, I'm not saying it isn't! So don't you feel just a bit sorry for Tullor?'

'No, I don't!' said Lizzy fervently. 'You didn't meet him before. You didn't see what he's like!'

'Maybe not. But he was only doing what the Queen told him to, wasn't he?'

'And enjoying every minute of it!'

'We don't know that for sure,' Rose argued. 'He was probably scared of her, like everyone else.' She shrugged. 'Oh, let's not talk about him any more. It's boring. Race you to the edge of the sea!'

Without waiting for Lizzy to reply, she sprinted off across the sand. For a moment or two Lizzy stood staring after her, feeling worried though she couldn't explain why even to herself. Then she pushed her thoughts away, and ran after Rose.

Hidden from view in his crevice, Tullor watched the aquarium visitors filing past his prison. He hated them all as much as ever. But now he had something else to think about. Something to *concentrate* on. And in his mind he formed a message.

Majesty . . . there is news. Good news. I think I have found a way to help you gain what you want . . .

He waited, hoping for the tingle in his consciousness that would tell him his mistress had heard his telepathic call.

After a little while, it came.

Chapter Two

As soon as the Baxters arrived home after their visit to the aquarium, Lizzy ran upstairs to her bedroom. She had promised Kes that she would contact him as soon as she could and reassure him that Tullor definitely was a prisoner.

On her dressing table was a large and beautiful spiral shell. Kes had given it to her when she first went under the sea with him, and to anyone else it simply looked like an ornament. But it was the twins' own very special way of communicating with each other.

Picking up the shell, Lizzy held it to her ear. At once she heard a soft, hissing surge, like the distant noise of the sea. She closed her eyes, concentrating hard, and after a few moments another sound began to mingle with the surge. A kind of singing or whistling, far away and haunting. Lizzy smiled as she recognized the voices of the dolphins calling to each other in their undersea home, and she whispered into the shell: '*Arhans . . .*' Arhans was the leader of the dolphins, and her special friend. '*Arhans, it's Lizzy . . . I want to see Kes and Morvyr. Meet me tomorrow morning. By the lighthouse . . .*' Concentrating hard, she pictured herself at the beach, with the sun climbing into the sky, then pictured a dolphin swimming towards her. '*Will you come, Arhans?*'

The whistling sounds paused for a moment, then swelled again in her ear. Lizzy was only just beginning to understand the dolphins' strange and alien language, but she felt in her mind that Arhans had heard her and understood.

She put the shell carefully back in its place and went downstairs.

Mum was getting tea ready, helped by Rose, and Lizzy said, 'Mum, I haven't got to do anything special tomorrow, have I?'

'Well, I'm not sure,' said Mum. 'We ought to make a start on sorting out all the things you need for your new school. If we don't do it soon, it'll be term-time before we know it. What did you want to do?'

'Oh, just go to the beach.'

Mum laughed. 'What, again? All right, then. But don't stay there all day.'

'OK. Thanks, Mum.' Lizzy went out of the kitchen. A minute later, Rose made an excuse to Mum and followed her.

'Are you meeting Kes tomorrow?' she asked, finding Lizzy in the sitting room.

'Yes,' said Lizzy. 'I want to tell him about Tullor.'

'Oh, right.' Rose paused, then added, 'Could I come with you?'

Lizzy paused, then sighed. 'Sorry, but . . . I think I ought to see him on my own.'

She left the room, and Rose stared after her, feeling disappointed and a little annoyed. Why was Lizzy so secretive? Rose knew about Kes and Morvyr now – for goodness' sake, she'd *seen* them for herself! – and she wanted to join in everything that happened from now on. But there were some things Lizzy still wanted to keep to herself. It was unkind of her, Rose thought. Unkind, and unfair.

Then something else occurred to her. How did Lizzy know that Kes would be at the beach to meet her? She couldn't exactly phone or text him when he lived under the sea! Had she fixed it up before they went to the aquarium, or was there some other, stranger answer?

Such as the shell that Lizzy kept in her bedroom . . .

The shell was an unusually large and beautiful spiral one, which Lizzy had found on the beach. Or so she said, though Rose was beginning to wonder if that was true. Once she had secretly followed Lizzy upstairs and had seen her put the shell to her lips and whisper to it. It was almost as if she were using it like a phone. Maybe, Rose thought, that was pretty close to the truth. It seemed fantastic and impossible, but could it be that Lizzy used the shell to communicate with her friends under the sea? And, if so, why hadn't Lizzy shared that part of the secret with her?

Suddenly she frowned and pinched the bridge of her nose. That weird dizzy spell at the aquarium had given her a headache. It had gone away, but now it was coming back again and making her irritable. Why did Lizzy have to be so mysterious? They were supposed to be good friends, and people didn't have secrets from their friends. Rose felt left out and rejected, and suddenly she was hit by a surge of anger. All right, if Lizzy wouldn't tell her what she wanted to know, then she'd find out for herself . . .

It was Lizzy's turn to wash up after tea, and when she had finished she said she was going to have a shower. Rose watched her hurry upstairs. She had taken a headache cure but it hadn't worked, and now she felt as if her whole head were buzzing like a hive full of bees. She couldn't stop thinking about the shell. The urge to investigate wouldn't leave her alone; in fact, it had grown so strong that it was almost a compulsion. And now she had her chance.

Upstairs, the bathroom door slammed. Rose didn't hesitate, but ran up to Lizzy's room, where she closed the door, picked the shell up and examined it. It seemed quite ordinary; it didn't rattle when she shook it, and there were no patterns on it that might be a code or something. Carefully Rose held it to her ear and heard a rushing, whispering noise, like the surge of waves breaking. She had expected that; she had learned long ago at school that it was just the echo of her own pulse. But there was nothing else.

Disappointed, she began to put the shell down again – then paused. There was another sound in her head; not just the surging but a sweeter noise, with a different rhythm. It sounded almost like a voice.

Eagerly Rose clamped the shell more firmly against her ear, straining to hear better. It *was* a voice! Lilting and beautiful, with a sing-song quality. Rose was fascinated. It was difficult to make out what the voice was saying, but after a few moments she heard a few words quite clearly.

'*Listen to me . . . Listen . . . Listen . . .*'

With a faraway look in her eyes, staring out of the window but seeing nothing, Rose listened.

Next morning Lizzy bolted her breakfast, to Mum's disapproval, then rushed upstairs for her beach bag. When she came down, she found Rose waiting for her in the hall.

'I'm coming to the beach too,' Rose said cheerfully.

'Oh.' Lizzy looked dismayed. 'Aren't you meeting Paul?'

'Not till later. I could do with a bit of sunbathing,

and maybe a swim.' Rose looked shrewdly at her. 'You don't mind, do you?'

Lizzie did mind, but couldn't very well say so. She was silent as they set off down through the narrow lanes towards the main street, then suddenly blurted, 'I didn't think you'd want to hang around with your kid sister!'

Rose laughed. 'Don't worry, I'm not going to. I'll just say hi to Kes, then you can have him all to yourself.'

'Right.' Lizzy nodded. 'The only thing is . . . I might not be meeting him actually *on* the beach.' There was a long pause, then she added, 'I'm going to see Morvyr too. And that means . . . well, she doesn't like coming close to shore.'

'Oh,' said Rose, understanding. 'You mean you're going out to sea to meet them?'

Another nod. They had reached the main street now, and turned away from the harbour and towards the beach. After another minute or so Rose said lightly, 'OK, it doesn't matter. Is it safe for you to go swimming, though? That mermaid –

Taran – I thought you said she was dangerous and she might be watching out for you?'

'I'll have Arhans with me,' Lizzy told her. 'I'll be safe with her.'

'Well, if you say so. Where are you meeting Kes and Morvyr, then?'

Rose's tone was light, but Lizzy detected something else in her voice. Rose seemed very keen to know exactly where she was going. And, for no reason that she could work out, Lizzy didn't want to tell her.

'I, um, don't know,' she said, trying to sound casual. 'Arhans will take me to them when we get out to sea.'

'Oh, come on! You *must* know, surely?'

'I don't.' Lizzy glanced sidelong at her sister and forced a smile. 'Sorry.'

Rose was obviously unconvinced, but she didn't ask any more questions until they reached the beach. The lifeguards were setting up for the day, though most of the summer holidaymakers hadn't arrived yet, and the only people in the sea were local surfers, looking like seals in their dark wetsuits.

Rose stopped on the sand and stared at the sea, fists on hips. 'I can't see your dolphin friend.'

'No, she'll be keeping out of sight. She's probably waiting over there somewhere.' Lizzy pointed to the end of the beach, where a low headland jutted out into the water. A small automatic lighthouse stood on the top, gleaming white in the early sun, and Lizzy headed towards a tumble of rocks at the headland's base. She hoped Rose would not follow her, but she was disappointed.

'So you're going to tell Kes and Morvyr about Tullor?' said Rose as she started to climb carefully over the rocks in Lizzy's wake. 'Will they have any news for you, do you think?'

'What sort of news?'

'I don't know. About Queen Taran, maybe. What she's doing now. They must have heard something.' Lizzy didn't answer, and after a few seconds Rose tried again. 'Couldn't Kes come here to meet you, so that I could hear the news too?'

Lizzy shook her head. 'It's already arranged.'

Rose sighed exasperatedly. 'I always seem to get left behind! I wish Jack Carrick hadn't gone fishing on the trawler with Paul and his dad. I bet he'd take me on the sailing-boat to see Morvyr if I asked him.'

'He might,' said Lizzy. 'I don't know.'

'Well, I think he would! And when he gets back, I'm going to – *ow*!' She stopped, clutching at a stubbed toe. 'These mussels are *sharp*! Why do all the rocks around here have to be covered in them?'

Rose's toe saved Lizzy from having to say anything else about meeting Morvyr, and she scrambled quickly to the top of the outcrop and gazed around. At first all she saw was the surf breaking over the rocks and the slow rise and fall of the swell. Then, a short way out, a curved fin broke the surface of the sea and a dolphin appeared. Lizzy recognized Arhans at once by the silver streak that ran the length of her back, and Arhans whistled a greeting and swam towards her.

By the time Rose had finished nursing her toe and climbed to the top, Lizzy was pulling on her wetsuit.

'There she is!' Rose's face broke into a smile of wonder. 'Isn't she beautiful? Arhans! Hello, Arhans! Do you remember me?' She reached out towards the dolphin and snapped her fingers as if she were beckoning to a dog.

'She isn't a pet!' Lizzy said sharply. 'And of course she remembers you.'

'All right, I only said – oh, forget it!' Rose's smile turned to a scowl, and she watched sullenly as Lizzy zipped up her wetsuit and stuffed her clothes into the beach bag. The resentment she had felt yesterday was surging back, and her head began to buzz again. It didn't hurt, but it irritated her, and she said snappishly, 'Look, what's the matter with you, Lizzy? You said you were going to tell me everything, but you've suddenly gone all secretive again, as if you don't want me to see Kes and Morvyr at all. I thought you trusted me!'

Lizzy had indeed promised to be honest with Rose – but there was one very important thing that she had *not* told her, and she wasn't quite sure why. In theory there should have been no harm in it. But an inner instinct was telling her that, at least for the time being, it would be safer for Rose not to know.

She met her sister's gaze and felt guilty. Rose looked lonely and forlorn and out of things. Surely it couldn't hurt to answer her question? But the instinct still said *no*, and she had to listen to it.

Lizzy sighed and said, 'I'm sorry. Really I am. I *do* trust you, of course I do, but there's a reason why I need to talk to Kes and Morvyr on my own. I can't tell you about it. As soon as I can, I will. But not yet.'

Rose sighed with exasperation. 'Oh, please yourself!' she retorted. 'Go off and have your secrets. But as soon as you *can* tell me, I want to know, all right?'

'All right.' Lizzy smiled a little sadly. 'Thanks, Rose.'

'Don't bother thanking me.' Rose bent to rub her sore toe again, her hair falling over her face. 'And don't expect me to cart your beach bag around for you all morning, because I won't!'

There was no reply, and Rose raised her head. Lizzy was no longer standing on the rock. Rose hadn't heard a splash, but in the space of a few seconds her sister had dived into the sea and vanished.

Rose stared at the tide slapping against the rocks, then scanned the water further out. No sign of Lizzy; no sign of a dolphin's fin. They were both gone.

She bit her lip, not knowing whether she felt angry, disappointed or just sad. Then she gave a sigh, picked up Lizzy's bag to place it safely above the high-tide mark and began to make her way cautiously back over the rocks to the sand.

Chapter Three

Lizzy's first breath underwater was always nerve-racking. She still found it hard to believe that she could do it, and there was an instant of heart-stopping fear as she opened her mouth and let the sea flow in. Then the bubbles streamed upwards past her face, she breathed a second time, and everything was all right.

She was still in the shallows, where the water was a beautiful shade of turquoise with sunlight glittering on the surface no more than a metre above her head. Arhans was waiting for her a short way off; her whistling call echoed eerily through the current, then she turned and led the way towards deeper water. Lizzy swam after her, moving quickly and easily, and gradually the colour around her changed to sapphire and then to a mysterious green-blue as they left the beach behind and swam out into the bay.

The sea teemed with life. There were fish everywhere, their scales winking like tiny diamonds. A huge crab scurried over the sandy bed below, almost loping along with its clumsy-looking sideways motion. A shoal of silvery mackerel darted across their path. Unable to resist the temptation Arhans snapped at them, but the fish scattered and dashed away, vanishing into the distance. The water became colder and the current stronger as they swam on, and the hiss and thunder of surf breaking on the shore gave way to the more muted rumble of the deep-sea tide. In the distance Lizzy could see the white wake of a motor boat, and heard the harsh chattering of its outboard engine as it sped by. It was probably one of the pleasure boats that took passengers out to watch seals and dolphins, and she smiled at the thought of what the people on board would think if they knew that a girl who was half mermaid was swimming almost under their noses.

They went on, Arhans surfacing every so often to breathe but taking care not to be seen by the boat trippers. Then another dolphin appeared and came towards them. Whistled greetings were exchanged before they veered away, leading Lizzy back in the direction of the shore.

She knew at once where they were going. There was a small, sandy inlet a little way up the coast, almost invisible until you were nearly on top of it. Kes and Morvyr were staying there for the time being, as the inlet was easier to protect from intruders or enemies than their undersea cave home. As they approached the rocks at the inlet's entrance there was a flurry of splashing ahead, and a voice called Lizzy's name.

'Kes!' She waved, and her brother came speeding to meet her. Though they were twins, the only remarkable likeness was in their vivid blue eyes, for

while Lizzy had the same pale blonde curls as
Morvyr, Kes had inherited the jet-black hair of their
human father, Jack Carrick. And, at least here
under the sea, there was another great difference
between them. Instead of human legs like Lizzy's,
Kes had a shining, fishlike green-blue tail.

He gave the tail a flip as he reached her and
somersaulted in the water amid a whirl of
bubbles, bringing himself to a stop. Grinning at
him, Lizzy felt a familiar pang of envy. Growing
up on land and knowing nothing about her
undersea heritage, she had never learned to
change her shape at will between human and
mermaid. To Kes it was second nature, but
though she had tried and tried and tried, Lizzy
couldn't make it happen. If it was a matter of
willpower, as Kes said, then it seemed Lizzy's
willpower just wasn't strong enough.

She pushed the regret away as Kes said, 'Arhans
told us you were coming. Mother's waiting in the
cove. Did you go to the aquarium?'

'Yes,' said Lizzy. 'Tullor's there, and it's all right

– he's in a glass tank and he can't possibly escape.'

Arhans made a chittering sound that seemed to express satisfaction, and Kes blew out his breath. 'I'm glad to hear that! Mother will be too. Come on, let's go to her. She's longing to see you.'

The two dolphins kept pace beside the twins as they swam towards the cliffs. The inlet was hard to spot at first, but Kes led the way unerringly to a narrow opening between rocks, and they swam through and into the cove.

Morvyr was waiting for them, seated on a rock with her mass of golden hair flowing over her shoulders. Her face lit when she saw Lizzy, and she hugged her tightly. 'Lizzy! Oh, how wonderful to see you!' Lizzy hugged her back and she went on eagerly, 'And your father – how is he?'

'He's gone to sea with Mr Treleaven,' Lizzy told her. 'I haven't heard from him yet, but he should be back in another day or two.' She settled on the rock beside Morvyr, and Kes climbed out of the water to join them. 'How are things here? Have you got any news?'

'No,' said Morvyr. 'Everything's fine.'

'Sort of,' Kes added.

Lizzy turned and looked at him curiously. 'Sort of? What do you mean? What's wrong?'

Kes hesitated, nibbling at his own lower lip. Then he said, 'Nothing's *wrong*. But that's what's bothering me. Everything's a bit too *right*.'

Lizzy looked blank and he continued, 'Mother and I are being very careful, in case Taran tries to kidnap us again to make Father give her the black pearl. That's why the dolphins are always on guard and we don't go anywhere without them to protect us. But it seems like there's nothing to protect us *from*. No one's heard anything about Taran since Tullor was caught, and none of her servants are around, either. It's all gone totally quiet.'

Lizzy began to see what he was getting at. 'And you don't trust it?' she asked.

'Too right, I don't! I think she's up to something. Trouble is, I don't know what.'

Lizzy looked questioningly at Morvyr, who

nodded. 'I agree with Kes, and so do the dolphins.' Her face was thoughtful. 'It's almost as if Taran has admitted defeat, but I know her better than that. She wants the black pearl, and she'll do anything to get it. Absolutely anything.'

'So you think she's got some new plan that she's working on, and that's why she's leaving you alone?'

'Yes. But as Kes said, we don't know what.'

'Well, at least she hasn't got Tullor to help her any more,' Lizzy said, trying to be reassuring. 'I saw him yesterday at the Sealife Centre. He's in a tank, and there's no way he can get out. And he was the worst of her henchmen, wasn't he?'

'Of course!' said Kes. 'I hadn't thought of that. Tullor did all her dirty work for her, didn't he? She used her magic to give him special powers. Perhaps *that's* why she's so quiet – she relied on him too much, and now she's stuck without him!'

'Perhaps,' Morvyr mused. 'Certainly her other servants are nowhere near as dangerous as Tullor was. But there could be another reason, and that's what worries me.' The twins looked at her curiously, and she lowered her voice and whispered, 'Karwynna.'

There was a sharp silence as Lizzy and Kes realized what she was getting at. This was the thing Lizzy had not told Rose, the secret that was known only to her sea family and the dolphins. Karwynna was the daughter of the old mermaid Queen, Kara, and thus the true heir to her crown. When Taran killed Kara and usurped the throne, Karwynna had disappeared, and for years the undersea people had believed she, too, must be dead. But when Morvyr had been held hostage in Taran's lair she had overheard Taran boasting to Tullor, and realized that Karwynna was still alive. Taran was holding her prisoner, but Morvyr did not know where. And that could be dangerous.

Morvyr voiced what they were all thinking. 'If Taran can't use us to get hold of the black pearl,' she said, 'then maybe she will try to use Karwynna.'

'You mean, bargain her in exchange for the

pearl?' Lizzy's face had paled. 'Oh, no . . . what would we *do*?'

'Karwynna is our rightful Queen.' Morvyr spread her hands helplessly. 'If it would save Karwynna's life, what *could* we do except give Taran the pearl?'

'But, Mother, would it save her?' Kes asked urgently. 'If Taran had the black pearl, her crown would be complete and she'd have total power! She wouldn't keep her side of the bargain, and there'd be nothing anyone could do about it!'

There was silence again as they all thought bleakly about what Kes had said. Then at last Morvyr spoke.

'Kes, my son, I'm afraid that what you say is true. Taran would not set Karwynna free. Why should she? She would have everything she ever wanted.'

'Then whatever happens, we *have* to make sure that she doesn't get the black pearl!' said Lizzy fiercely.

'You're right, Lizzy. So we must wait for your

father to return, and when he does, we must all meet again and decide what to do.'

Arhans whistled forceful agreement, and Lizzy said uneasily, 'But what *can* we do?'

'I don't know.' Morvyr shivered. 'But there must be a way to outwit her. We mustn't let her win. We *mustn't*!'

They talked for a while longer before Lizzy said that she ought to get back to the beach in case anyone went looking for her. She promised Morvyr that as soon as the *Regard*, Mr Treleaven's trawler, came home, she would contact Jack and arrange for them all to meet again.

Arhans was ready to escort her to shore, and Morvyr gave Kes permission to go too. As they swam back, Lizzy was thinking about Taran and what she might be planning. And then she remembered something.

'Kes . . .' She stopped, treading water and back-finning with her hands to stay in place. 'I didn't tell you before, but – something a bit strange happened at the aquarium.'

'Oh?' Kes frowned. 'What?'

She told him about the dizzy spell Rose had had while she was looking at Tullor. 'Mum and Dad thought it was because of the weird light in there, and the enclosed space and that sort of thing. But . . . well, it isn't like Rose to do that.'

Kes considered, while Arhans swam in lazy circles around them. Then he said, 'I don't think it's anything to worry about. Like your parents said: weird light, and all closed in –' He shuddered. 'I'd *hate* that. It must be really horrible, and I'm not surprised Rose went funny.'

'Then you don't think Tullor might have had anything to do with it?'

He shook his head. 'Nah. How could he have done?'

Lizzy was relieved. She hadn't really thought, herself, that there was anything suspicious about it. But all the same it was reassuring to know that Kes agreed.

The beach was soon in sight. Kes didn't want to come too close to shore in case anyone saw him in his merboy form, so he and Lizzy said goodbye and he headed back for the cove with Arhans. Lizzy picked a quiet spot to wade out of the sea – she didn't want the lifeguards to see her – and was glad to find that Rose was nowhere around. However, she discovered her beach bag on a rock clear of the tide, and changed her wetsuit for shorts and T-shirt before walking slowly home.

She wasn't worried about the incident at the Sealife Centre. It was just one of those things, she was sure. But something else *was* bothering her. Rose had started to ask more questions than usual. Mostly they were just trivial things, like today when she had wanted to know exactly where Lizzy was meeting Kes and Morvyr. But it didn't seem quite natural.

Or was she imagining it? Lizzy didn't know. But she felt slightly uneasy, and decided that it might be a good idea to take more notice of what Rose said or did. Just in case.

Chapter Four

There was no doubt about it, Lizzy soon realized: the intensity of Rose's sudden interest wasn't quite natural. OK, it was understandable that she should want to know what was happening, but this was getting crazy. She was asking so *many* questions. And she no longer became huffy or annoyed when Lizzy refused to tell her something. Instead, she just let the subject drop for a while, then asked again in a slightly different way. She was very, very persistent.

Two days later the *Regard* was still not back, and Lizzy was growing impatient. She needed to talk to Jack and she wanted to ask his advice. Kes had told her not to worry about Rose, but Lizzy knew her sister very well, and she was convinced there was more to this than met the eye.

Then, for no apparent reason, Rose mentioned the Isles of Scilly.

'I'd really love to go there,' she remarked when the family were all together that evening. 'It's supposed to be a cool place. There are helicopter day trips, or you can go on the ferry.'

'You'd get seasick,' said Mum. 'Anyway, the islands probably aren't much different to Cornwall. They're only about thirty miles from Land's End, after all.'

'What's with the sudden interest, anyway?' Dad asked.

Rose shrugged carelessly. 'Oh, I was just reading something about it. You know.'

Lizzy said nothing. But she noticed that Rose just happened to mention the islands several more times that evening. There was something else too. Someone had been moving her shell. She knew because she was supposed to tidy her own room.

Tidying included dusting, but Lizzy was so eager to get the chore out of the way and do something more interesting that she usually 'forgot'. As a result, her shelves gathered a fine film of dust before she guiltily got round to cleaning them. So it was easy to see the tell-tale clean patches that showed where the shell had been picked up and then put down again in a slightly different place.

If Mum had moved the shell, she would have dusted the shelf and ticked Lizzy off for not doing it herself. So it had to be Rose. But why? Lizzy had never told her how she could use the shell to make contact with the undersea world. So what could Rose possibly want with it? It was baffling.

She was still puzzling over the mystery when, at breakfast next morning, Dad began grumbling that he needed a break.

'Poor old Dad.' Rose grinned at him. 'All that paperwork for the new college year getting to you, is it? Now you know what it's like for us at school! Doesn't he, Lizzy?'

'Mmm?' Lizzy wasn't really listening.

'Wake up, dreamy! Dad just said he's fed up with work, so *I* said −'

Mum interrupted. 'Well, I don't see why he shouldn't have a break. In fact, why we all shouldn't. We've got enough time before the new term starts, and I could arrange a few days off.' She looked questioningly at Mr Baxter. 'What do you reckon? Shall we book ourselves a last-minute holiday somewhere?'

Horrified, Lizzy was about to protest, but before she could say anything Rose jumped in.

'That'd be brilliant!' she enthused. 'And I know the perfect place − the Isles of Scilly!'

Lizzy froze with her mouth open. Mum and Dad were both looking vaguely interested, and Rose, her eyes alight, went on. 'It's ideal, because it's not far away, and we wouldn't have to bother about foreign currency or passports; we could just pack some stuff and get on the ferry! Oh, let's go there!'

'Hang on, hang on!' said Dad. 'We don't know if we're going anywhere yet!'

'You just said −'

'I know I did, and it'd be great. But wouldn't you rather pick somewhere more exciting? A city break, maybe; Paris or –'

Rose shook her head. 'Who wants to go to Paris in August? It'd be boiling! I'd rather be by the sea.'

'You're by the sea here,' Mum pointed out. 'The Isles of Scilly would be more of the same. And there isn't much to do there; no big towns or shops.'

'I don't care,' said Rose. 'I vote for Scilly!'

Mum looked at Dad, who shrugged. 'If Rose is that keen, why not?' he said cheerfully. 'So long as I don't have to do any work, I don't mind where we go.'

'It's still high season, remember,' said Mum. 'We don't know if we'll be able to get in anywhere at such short notice.'

Rose wasn't put off. 'There must be somewhere,' she said eagerly. 'Look, I've got some brochures in my room. I'll get them and we can look on the Internet and see what's available.'

Without waiting for an answer she ran out and the others heard her pounding upstairs.

Dad raised his eyebrows. 'I've never seen Rose so keen!'

'Well, if it's all right with you, it's fine with me,' said Mum. 'The only thing is, no one's asked Lizzy what she thinks.' She looked at Lizzy. 'Would *you* like to have a few days on the Isles of Scilly, Lizzy?'

Lizzy's pulse was beating fast. Rose was up to something – she was certain of it. And there was a connection with the islands.

'Yes,' she said. 'I'd love to.'

Astonishingly, by lunchtime it was all arranged. Rose had come rushing downstairs again with a sheaf of brochures that she must have picked up at the local Tourist Information office, and it only took a short search on the Internet and a few phone calls to find a self-catering cottage that had just had a last-minute cancellation. Another phone call booked their places on the Scillonian ferry for the coming Thursday, and that was that.

The cottage was on St Agnes, the smallest of the five inhabited islands. Studying a map that had come with her brochures, Rose said that there were lots of beaches and a separate small island that you could reach by a sandy causeway at low tide. 'It's really quiet,' she said enthusiastically. 'Perfect!'

To call a quiet place 'perfect' was so unlike Rose that Lizzy's suspicion deepened. *Perfect for what?* she wondered. What *was* going on in Rose's mind? If only Jack would come back! She needed to tell him about this.

Halfway through the afternoon Lizzy's mobile rang and, when she looked at the screen and saw who was calling, her heart gave a jump.

'Jack!' There was relief and delight in her voice. 'Where are you?'

'We've just put in to port,' said Jack. 'How's things?'

'Fine – well, that is, except . . .' But it was impossible to explain over the phone, when her family might overhear. 'Could I meet you at the harbour?' she asked.

'Sure, no problem. Give us an hour or so to unload our catch and get the boat sorted, and I'll be free.'

'Brilliant!'

'I wouldn't be surprised if Kes turns up as well.' Jack laughed. 'Arhans escorted us home, and I think she's gone to tell him.'

'That's even better! OK, see you soon.'

Lizzy couldn't bear to wait a whole hour and set off for the harbour too early. She was so wrapped up in working out what she needed to tell Jack and how she would say it that she had gone several hundred metres down the road before she realized she had left her purse at home. She wanted something from one of the local shops . . . Well, she had lots of time before Jack would be finished on the *Regard*. If she went back and got the purse, her timing should be just right.

She hurried back home and let herself in. Mum and Dad were both out, but as Lizzy closed the front door she heard Rose's voice. It was coming from upstairs, and Lizzy's first thought was that

Rose was talking to a friend on her mobile. But then, as she was about to rush noisily up the stairs, Lizzy paused. Who *was* Rose talking to? There was something strange about her voice. She sounded detached, almost dreamy. People didn't talk to their friends like that.

Suddenly Lizzy's misgivings came back and, instead of running, she crept upstairs on silent feet and stopped on the landing. She could hear Rose more clearly now. And she wasn't in her own room. She was in Lizzy's.

A cold, prickling feeling washed over Lizzy and made her shiver. She tiptoed along the landing and stopped again just before she reached her room. Rose had stopped talking, and Lizzy cautiously leaned forward until she could peer round the half-open door.

Rose was standing by the window. She had her back to Lizzy and she was holding the shell to her ear. Her head was on one side, as if she were listening intently, and as Lizzy watched she said, 'Yes . . . St Agnes. We're going on Thursday . . .

that's in three days.' She still sounded dreamy, and there was a pause as she listened again. 'Yes. Yes, I will. I promise. I'll be there . . . Yes, I'll be very careful.'

She started to lower the shell, and hastily Lizzy backed away. She returned to the stairs, went halfway down, then came up again making as much noise as usual. By the time she reached the top, Rose was on the landing as though she had just emerged from her own room.

'Forgot my purse!' Lizzy smiled at her, hoping it looked convincing.

'Oh, right.' Rose headed for the staircase. By the time Lizzy had retrieved her purse she was in the kitchen, apparently busy and humming a tune to herself.

'See you later,' Lizzy said.

Rose did not ask where she was going. She just said vaguely, 'What? Oh – yeah, sure. Have fun,' and started humming again.

Lizzy went out into the street. She had proof now. Rose must have spied on her, and had worked out that the shell was a way of communicating with her friends in the sea. But who was she talking to just now? Not Kes or the dolphins, that was for sure. Who, then?

An awful thought began to dawn in Lizzy's mind. Could Rose's mysterious contact be Taran? She told herself that the idea was totally crazy – the mermaid Queen couldn't possibly have found a way of reaching Rose. She didn't have any spies on land.

Except one, said a silent inner voice.

Lizzy's eyes widened as she recalled Rose's dizzy spell at the Sealife Centre. *Could* there be a connection? Could Tullor have used some kind of telepathy to reach out to Rose's mind and affect her?

Lizzy's heart started to bump under her ribs and she pushed down a sick feeling. Some pieces of the puzzle were starting to fit horribly into place. And it was all connected with the coming trip to the Isles of Scilly . . .

She turned and started to run as fast as she could towards the harbour.

Chapter Five

The *Regard* was moored up at the fish dock. The unloading of the catch was almost complete, supervised by Mr Treleaven, and as she gazed around Lizzy saw Jack standing a little way off near the covered market. Kes was with him.

'Lizzy!' Jack's black-bearded face beamed as he saw her too. Lizzy ran to join them and Jack clapped a hand each on her and Kes's shoulders. 'It's good to see you both!' he said. Then he saw Lizzy's expression and his look changed. 'What is it? Is something wrong?'

'Lizzy?' Kes was looking enquiringly at her too.

'Has something else happened?' Lizzy hesitated and he added, 'Is it Rose?'

Lizzy nodded sombrely. 'I don't know for sure,' she said, 'but I think Taran's got at her.'

For a moment there was silence, then Jack said, 'Look, let's move away from here to somewhere more private. Then I think you'd better tell us.'

They walked in the direction of the lifeboat station and sat down on a low wall that overlooked the inner harbour.

'Right,' said Jack. 'Lizzy, when I rang you earlier, you said everything was fine, "except" . . . What did you mean, "except"?'

Lizzy told Jack about the incident at the aquarium. There was something else she had forgotten until now, and she added that Rose had said later that she 'felt sorry' for Tullor.

'*Sorry* for him?' Kes echoed explosively. 'How could anyone feel *sorry*? She must be totally crazy!'

'Wait a minute, Kes.' Jack held up a hand. 'I agree, it's a strange thing for anyone to think. So maybe we should ask ourselves why Rose thought it?' He paused, then: 'Lizzy, has Rose said anything else about Tullor since then?'

Lizzy shook her head. 'No. But these last few days she's started acting weirdly.' She explained it all: the questions Rose had begun asking, her sudden obsession with the Isles of Scilly and, most important of all, how she had seen her sister whispering into the shell. Jack and Kes listened without interrupting, and when Lizzy finished Jack let out a long, whistling breath.

'Did you know about this, Kes?' he asked.

Kes shook his head. 'Lizzy told Mother and me about Rose getting dizzy,' he said, 'but I hadn't heard the rest until now.' His face reddened. 'I didn't think the aquarium business was important, so I said Lizzy shouldn't worry about it.'

'Hmm. Well, I'm sorry to say I think you were wrong,' said Jack. 'I have a nasty feeling that Taran *is* behind this, and she used Tullor to help her make contact with Rose.'

'But how?' Kes asked. 'He's a prisoner. She can't reach him.'

'Not physically, no,' said Jack. 'But she might still have a link with his mind, and she could have used him to hypnotize Rose, so that she could take control of her through the shell. Tullor's no ordinary conger eel, remember – Taran gave him powers that other creatures don't have.' He paused. 'Then there's the Isles of Scilly connection.'

'Connection?' Lizzy and Kes were puzzled.

'Oh, yes. Do you remember when you took the silver pearl to Taran? You both went through the magical gateway which led to the rainbow pool in the cave of mirrors under the sea. That's the Queen's court, where Taran lives now. It's the focus of her power. And it's very close to the islands.'

Kes's eyes lit with understanding. 'That's why Taran wants Rose to have this holiday – it's the perfect place to arrange a meeting without having to go far from her lair!'

'But why would she want to meet Rose?' Lizzy asked. 'What's she planning?'

'I think that's easy to answer,' said Jack. 'Taran

wants Rose to steal the black pearl and give it to her.'

Lizzy was horrified. 'She can't – she wouldn't!'

'She would if Taran hypnotized her,' Kes pointed out grimly.

'Then we've got to stop her! I'm going to tell her we know what Taran's up to –'

'No, Lizzy,' Jack interrupted. 'That would be a big mistake. If Rose has been hypnotized, chances are she isn't even aware of the things she's doing. If you confront her, she'll say you're crazy and Taran will soon realize that we've found out the truth.'

'But Rose might be in danger!' Lizzy persisted.

'Don't worry, she isn't. I'm sure of that. And I've got another idea. One that could help us lure Taran into a trap.'

'What sort of a trap?' Lizzy asked dubiously.

Jack stood up. 'Before I tell you, I think we all ought to talk to Morvyr. Kes, you go back to her now, and when I've helped Jeff finish everything on the *Regard* I'll borrow his sailing-boat and bring Lizzy to the cove.'

'All right, Father,' said Kes. 'But can't you tell us the plan now?'

'Not yet. I need to work it out properly first.' Jack smiled reassuringly. 'I know it's hard, but you'll just have to be patient!'

When Morvyr heard Lizzy's story, she was very troubled.

'We thought that Taran must be plotting something,' she said, 'but I didn't expect this. Poor Rose – and poor Lizzy too; it must be so worrying for you!'

She was on the rock in the cove again with Kes beside her, while Lizzy and Jack sat in the small sailing-boat *Silvie*. Arhans, too, was with them and was swimming slowly around the boat. She had made no comment yet but she was listening carefully.

'Father says Rose probably doesn't know that Taran's got power over her,' Kes told Morvyr. 'Lizzy wanted to confront her, but he said no.' He glanced at Jack. 'He's got a plan, but he wanted to see you before he tells us about it.'

Morvyr looked at Jack too, questioningly, and Jack said, 'It's to do with the magical gateways that lead to the rainbow pool. The black pearl's gate is near the Isles of Scilly, isn't it?'

'Yes,' said Morvyr. 'It's the most powerful one of all.'

'And the only one that Taran can't control – which is why she's so eager for Rose and Lizzy to go there. If she can get her hands on the black pearl, she'll be able to open that last gateway.'

'And that will restore the full strength of the crown.' Morvyr's grey eyes clouded with fear and anger. 'No one will be able to stand against her then.'

'So we must make sure that doesn't happen. Which is where my plan comes in.' Jack smiled at Lizzy and Kes. 'I'm sorry I was so secretive earlier, but there was something I needed to find before I told you about it.'

'Did you find it?' Kes asked.

'Oh, yes.' Jack thrust a hand into his jeans

pocket and took out a handkerchief, tightly folded into a small wad. The others watched silently as he unwrapped it, and as the last fold fell away they all gasped.

Inside the handkerchief was the black pearl.

Morvyr was horrified. 'Jack, what have you done?' she gasped. 'It should be kept safe in the locket!'

Jack was grinning. 'I was just testing to see if it would fool you, and it did. Don't worry. This is *not* the real black pearl.'

Morvyr's alarm turned to wonder and, hesitant, she reached out and touched the pearl with a fingertip. 'But it looks exactly the same!' she said. 'I couldn't have told the difference!'

'Then I've obviously done a good job.' Jack's grin broadened. 'This is a perfectly ordinary pearl. A large one, I admit, but there's nothing magical about it.'

'Where did you get it?' Lizzy asked.

'When I was rescued from the French trawler a few weeks ago, I was wearing a belt-pouch,' he told her. 'It didn't have much in it, just a few coins and one or two little souvenirs I'd picked up on my travels. Including this. I bought it from a pearl-diver in the Far East – oh, years ago – and kept it as a sort of good-luck charm. I put it away in a drawer when I moved in with the Treleavens. So before I came out here I found it, painted it black and added a bit of silver to give it a shine.'

'It's astonishing,' said Morvyr. 'Just like the real one.'

'If you think that, then so will Taran. And we're going to use it to set a trap for her.'

'How?' Kes asked eagerly.

'Right,' said Jack, 'this is the plan. Lizzy, could I borrow your locket for a minute?'

Puzzled and intrigued, she took it off and handed it to him. Jack opened it, then unlocked the secret compartment. For years the silver pearl had been hidden there; now, though, Taran had the pearl and the compartment was empty. Carefully Jack placed the fake black pearl inside.

'There,' he said. 'A perfect fit.' He closed the

locket and gave it back to Lizzy. 'Now, I'll bet you anything that Rose will soon ask you – very casually – where the black pearl is. When she does, I want you to tell her that it's safe inside your locket. And, of course, when you go to the Isles of Scilly, you'll take the locket with you.'

Lizzy saw what he had in mind. 'Then, when we're there, Rose will steal the locket, with the fake pearl in it, and arrange to meet Taran and give it to her!'

'Exactly. You'll have to make it easy for her without raising her suspicions, but that shouldn't be a problem.'

'And when she goes to meet Taran,' Kes chimed in excitedly, 'we'll all be waiting, and we'll get her!'

Jack laughed. 'Well, not quite, Kes! It'll be a bit more complicated than that. But the first part of the trap will be laid. And now I'll tell you the rest . . .'

They all leaned forward, huddling together, and Arhans nosed in too as Jack began to explain in detail.

Chapter Six

'Sure you've got everything?' Rose asked as she struggled down the stairs with her holdall.

Lizzy was waiting in the hall with her own lightweight bag. 'That's the hundredth time you've asked me,' she said. 'The way you talk, anyone'd think we were going away for five months, not five days.'

Rose reached the hall and thankfully dropped the holdall with a thud on the floor. 'I know what you're like, that's all.'

'Well, I've got my wetsuit and mobile phone, and they're the only really important things.'

'Yeah, till you find out you've forgotten to pack

a swimsuit, or sandals, or clean underwear, or your locket or something.' Rose paused, then added in a deliberately casual way, 'You are taking your locket, aren't you?'

'I'm wearing it.' Lizzy tugged on the silver chain round her neck and showed Rose the locket. 'Why?'

She knew perfectly well why Rose was so concerned about the locket, but she couldn't resist asking the question. Rose shrugged and said, 'Well, you don't want to leave it behind, not with the black pearl inside. Imagine if we had a burglary while we were away.'

Or imagine if you arranged to meet Taran and then couldn't get hold of the pearl, Lizzy thought.

Mum came down the stairs then, carrying her own bag. 'Are you girls ready?' she asked. 'We've got to leave in five minutes, or we'll be late for the ferry.'

'We've got everything,' said Rose. 'But I don't know where Dad is.'

Mrs Baxter raised her eyebrows heavenward. 'If

he hasn't finished packing . . . Mark!' she called in the direction of Dad's study. 'Mark, hurry up!'

'Coming!' Dad appeared from the study. 'I was just making sure everything's switched off that needs to be. Right, Mum can bring the car round, and I'll take the bags outside.' He picked up Rose's holdall. 'Good grief, Rose, what have you got in here? It weighs half a ton.'

'Just clothes and stuff,' Rose said huffily.

And something else? Lizzy wondered. She hadn't checked her room since Rose came downstairs, but . . .

'I'm going to the loo,' she said aloud. 'In case we have to wait ages at the ferry.'

'Well, buck up,' said Mum. 'Or we really will be late!' She went out to get the car, and Dad began lugging the bags to the front door. Rose followed him, and Lizzy dashed upstairs. But she didn't go to the bathroom. Instead, she peered round the door of her own bedroom.

As she had expected, her shell wasn't there. So Rose had sneaked in at the last minute and taken it, and now no doubt it was carefully wrapped up inside her holdall. Any doubts Lizzy might have had about her suspicions faded and vanished. Rose and Taran were in league with each other. And the plan that Jack had prepared would very soon be put into action.

A car horn beeped, and hastily Lizzy ran down the stairs and outside.

Despite Mum's worries they were at the Penzance quay in plenty of time and, with their bags safely stowed in the metal luggage containers, they walked up the gangplank of the Scillonian ferry. The weather was still lovely, and Dad suggested finding outside seats on deck, where they would have a glorious view. Rose, remembering how seasick she had been on the *Regard*, would have preferred to go inside to the passenger lounge, but she was outvoted.

The ferry was fully booked and the deck was crowded with happily chattering people. Mum soon got talking to a couple in the seats behind them, and Dad made himself comfortable and opened his daily newspaper. Soon the boat moved slowly away from the quay and turned towards the open sea. Lizzy leaned on the rail beside her seat. She wondered if she might see Arhans and her friends, but as yet there was no sign of them. Perhaps, she thought, they were already escorting Kes and Morvyr to the islands, in which case they would arrive before the ferry did. And Jack was flying out by helicopter later this morning. It was frustrating, but for now there was nothing Lizzy could do except wait, and try to forget her nervousness enough to enjoy the voyage.

The journey was uneventful, apart from a return of Rose's seasickness. Mum bought her a packet of ginger sweets from the onboard shop – ginger, she said, was very good for sickness – and Rose retreated to the covered lounge, where she fell asleep for a while on one of the cushioned seats. The rest of the Baxters stayed outside, looking at the sea and breathing the salty wind that whipped their hair as the boat powered onwards. Patches of summery white cloud scudded across the sky, the lonely Wolf Rock lighthouse slid by on the port side, and then there was nothing but the glittering blue-green sea stretching away in every direction.

As the sun climbed towards its highest point the Isles of Scilly appeared on the horizon, and before long the boat was easing gently into St Mary's harbour. Again Lizzy looked eagerly for signs of dolphins, but again there was nothing.

Rose was feeling better, and while the Baxters waited for their luggage to be transferred to the smaller boat that would take them on to St Agnes she went to a nearby shop and came back with a large bar of chocolate and two magazines. Lizzy gazed around, wondering if Jack had arrived and where he was staying. Then they were climbing aboard the waiting catamaran, and with a roar and chatter of the engine they powered away from the harbour.

During the next two hours Lizzy was too caught

up in the excitement of arriving and settling in to think about anything else. A small tractor with a trailer behind it was waiting at the quay, and their luggage was taken on ahead while they strolled to the holiday cottage. The cottage was small but comfortable. The bedroom that Lizzy and Rose were to share had a wonderful view of the sea, and a big box of groceries had been left for them in the kitchen.

The island itself was surprisingly different from the mainland. It was quite low-lying, with wide expanses of turfy grass and heather. There were no trees of any size, just low-growing bushes, and strangely shaped rock formations, smoother and more rounded than those on their own coast, rose out of the ground like prehistoric creatures emerging from the earth. More rounded rocks fringed the beaches and little lagoons, and a small lighthouse, now disused, stood on one of the highest points, gleaming white in the sun.

Rose wanted to start exploring at once, but Mum said firmly that no one was going anywhere until they had unpacked properly and had some lunch. Rose gave way, but Lizzy sensed how impatient she was as they prepared and ate sandwiches.

As soon as lunch was finished Rose jumped to her feet and said, 'I'm going to go and explore.'

'All right,' said Mum. 'I expect Lizzy'd like to go with you. Wouldn't you, Lizzy?'

Rose and Lizzy looked at each other, and Lizzy saw complete dismay on Rose's face.

'Mum and I are off to the nearest beach, with a rug and a couple of good books,' said Dad. 'While this weather lasts, we're going to make the most of it.'

Lizzy smiled innocently at Rose. 'I think I'll come with you, Dad,' she said. 'I'm feeling lazy too. I might go for a walk later.'

Rose visibly relaxed. 'OK, cool,' she said. And she went before Lizzy could change her mind.

By evening, Lizzy had made some explorations of her own and was starting to find her way around.

Though the island was not much more than a kilometre long, it had so many beaches that it was impossible to guess where Rose and Taran might arrange to meet. Many of the beaches were rocky and difficult to walk on, but others had stretches of smooth, silvery sand. One place in particular would be ideal: a sandy causeway that joined the main part of St Agnes to a smaller island called the Gugh. The water here was calm and the beach shelved gently on both sides. Lizzy wondered if Rose had seen it.

Rose did not say much about where she had been and what she had found, but she seemed pleased. No one felt like cooking, so they walked to the island's one pub and had a meal there, then returned to the cottage in the afterglow of a glorious sunset. Everyone was tired by this time, and no one argued when Mum suggested an early night.

If sharing a room with Lizzy was going to make Rose's plans difficult, Rose showed no sign of it. When both the girls were in bed, she reached to switch off the light, then suddenly paused and said, 'Your locket's safe, isn't it?'

'Yes, of course it is,' Lizzy replied.

'And the black pearl's still in there?'

'Yeah.' Lizzy sounded casual. 'I checked.'

'Great.' Rose flicked the light switch, added, 'Night', and turned over, pulling her duvet up around her ears. Lizzy lay still, watching the cool silver light reflecting from the sea and wondering if Rose was really going to sleep or pretending. She had sent a text message to Jack but he had not replied yet. She wondered where he was. And Kes and Morvyr – were they here? She had no way of knowing.

For a while there were small noises below, then Lizzy heard the creak of the stairs as Mum and Dad came up to their bedroom. Their low voices murmured for a few more minutes, then everything was quiet. Lizzy waited. And after another half hour, her patience was rewarded when Rose slid out of bed.

Peeking through half-closed eyelids, Lizzy

watched as her sister padded across the room. Rose bent to her bag and took out Lizzy's shell. She turned to look at Lizzy, and quickly Lizzy shut her eyes completely. Then she heard the faint click of the old-fashioned door latch lifting, and opened her eyes again just in time to see Rose tiptoeing out of the room.

She sat upright. Dared she follow? Reluctantly she decided it was safer not to. If Rose should see her, it would ruin everything. So instead she got out of bed and went to the window. The cottage had a front door and a side door, and if Rose went out of either, Lizzy would be able to see her.

Sure enough, a few moments later the side door opened and Rose appeared. She glanced up at the window – Lizzy dodged back behind the curtain – then hurried down the short front-garden path to the gate. The sea beyond was steeped in moonlight, and Rose's figure showed clearly against the silvery background. She walked a few steps clear of the garden, then put the shell to her ear.

From this distance Lizzy could not hear what

Rose said, but she had no doubt that she was talking to Taran. So it was really beginning . . . Her heart gave an uncomfortable lurch of nervous excitement, then as Rose lowered the shell and turned back towards the cottage, she hurried to bed once more.

When Rose crept upstairs and got into her own bed, Lizzy's eyes were closed and she was breathing steadily. Rose wriggled under the duvet and was soon fast asleep.

But Lizzy lay awake for a long time, wondering what would happen tomorrow.

Chapter Seven

It was only just getting light when Lizzy woke the next morning. Rose was still sleeping, and she dressed quickly and quietly then hurried downstairs. Sometime during the night she thought she had heard a muffled signal from her mobile phone, which was under her pillow, telling her that a text message had come in, and she wanted to be alone to read it in case it was from Jack.

In the kitchen, though, she found that Dad was up before her.

'Hello, you're an early riser!' Dad was pouring milk on a bowl of cereal.

'Oh – hi, Dad. Yes, I woke up, and it's such a lovely day I didn't want to waste any of it.' Lizzy glanced surreptitiously at her phone, and saw Jack's name on the display screen. Her heart skipped.

'Good for you. Want some of this?' Dad waved the cereal packet.

'Er . . . yes, please. Could you do it for me? I've just got to check something.' Lizzy turned her back and touched buttons. Jack's text message was very short.

Will b at jetty early. See u there. J.

'Got a message?' Dad asked.

'Just – um – one of my friends,' said Lizzy vaguely. Did Jack mean he was coming to St Agnes? How would he get here? And what did he call early? She looked at her watch and saw that it wasn't even six thirty. He surely wouldn't be here yet; and anyway, he would wait for her. She just had to make sure that she got out of the cottage and away before Rose woke up.

'There you go.' Dad put her cereal on the table

and plonked a spoon beside it. Lizzy ate quickly, then said, 'I think I'll go for a walk. Won't be very long.'

'OK.' Dad was trying to decide between jam and marmalade to put on his toast. 'Don't get lost, or we'll have to send out a search party!'

They both laughed, and Lizzy hurried out.

In fact Lizzy did get lost. Taking what she thought was a short cut to the jetty, she chose the wrong path and ended up beside a large, almost circular pool, beyond which a rocky finger of land with what looked like ruined walls on it reached out into the sea. From here she couldn't work out where the jetty was, and she wasted more time dithering over which path to try. At last, though, a holidaymaking couple taking their dog for an early walk pointed her in the right direction, and she ran all the way, finally arriving hot and breathless.

A small motor launch was moored beside the jetty, and, shading her eyes against the early sun, Lizzy saw a familiar figure sitting in it.

'Jack!' Relief filled her and she ran down the slope to the boat.

'You got my message!' Jack grinned at her. 'I wasn't sure if I'd done it properly; I'm not used to texting yet!'

'When did you get here?' Lizzy asked. 'And have you seen Kes and Morvyr? Or the dolphins?'

'Yesterday, no and yes.' His grin broadened. 'I'm staying on St Mary's, and I've hired this boat.' He patted the steering wheel in front of him. 'It's got an inboard engine and it's much faster than a sailing-boat. Perfect for what we want. Now, I saw Arhans yesterday, just before it got dark. She came on ahead of the other dolphins – they were escorting Kes and Morvyr and travelling overnight, so they're probably here by now. What about you? Has anything happened?'

Lizzy described how Rose had taken the shell and crept outside last night. Jack nodded. 'So Taran knows she's here. And Rose definitely thinks you've got the black pearl?'

Lizzy nodded. 'She asked me about it again before we went to sleep.'

'Good. Taran's very impatient – I don't think we'll have to wait long before they make their move.'

In the distance there was a ripple on the sea, and a sleek grey fin broke the surface and came speeding towards them. Whistling a greeting, Arhans swam up to the launch, and Lizzy leaned down to stroke her smooth head.

'Arhans! Are the others here?'

Arhans whistled again, and Jack said, 'She says they're waiting not far away. Come on, Lizzy – jump in, and she'll take us to them.'

Lizzy scrambled down into the boat. Jack started the engine, and they followed Arhans as she swam away from the jetty and out to open water. Bearing away to the right, she led them round the Gugh until they reached a large inlet on the far side of the sand causeway.

'I came here yesterday, when I was exploring,'

Lizzy told Jack. 'I think it's a pretty likely place for Taran to meet Rose, don't you?'

'I'm not so sure,' said Jack. 'If I know Taran, I think she'll pick somewhere a bit more remote. But we'll have to wait and see. Ah – look! There they are!'

Kes was waving from the beach at the far end of the sandbar. In the water a few metres out they could see the pale gold of Morvyr's hair. Jack swung the boat towards the bar, and within a minute Lizzy was jumping out into the shallows and running to greet her mother and brother.

'That was some swim from the mainland!' Kes said, grinning at her. 'But the dolphins helped us. Is there any news?'

Lizzy repeated what she had already told Jack.

'Good,' said Morvyr. 'So now we must wait for Taran. No one's seen her yet, but Kes and I had better keep out of sight until we know exactly where she is. You too, Jack – if she realizes that you're here, she'll be suspicious.'

Jack nodded. 'I'll go back to St Mary's. It

wouldn't do for Rose to see me, either. The dolphins will keep us in touch with one another, and I can contact Lizzy by phone as soon as anything happens.' Now he turned to Lizzy. 'In some ways, Lizzy, yours is the hardest task. You've got to stick around with Rose and act as though everything's perfectly normal. Can you do that?'

'I'm sure I can,' Lizzy said, then added more honestly, 'I'll do my very best, anyway.'

'That's the girl! So, we'll all go our separate ways now, and wait.'

'How long do you think we'll have to wait, Father?' Kes asked. 'When do you think Taran will make her move?'

'I don't know,' Jack replied. 'But I wouldn't mind betting it'll be tonight . . .'

Chapter Eight

Rose was very jumpy that evening. Mum and Dad didn't seem to notice, but Lizzy did. Rose kept glancing at her when she thought no one was looking, and Lizzy noticed the way her sister's eyes always fixed on the locket round her neck. It told her all she needed to know. Rose was trying to work out a way of persuading Lizzy to take the locket off so that she could get hold of it, and she was getting more and more agitated. That could mean only one thing – she and Taran planned to meet tonight.

All right, Lizzy thought, then she would make things easier for Rose. Dinner that evening was a simple pizza and salad, and afterwards Mum and Dad decided to stroll to the pub, where they could sit outside and watch the sunset. When they asked the girls if they would like to come, Rose said she wanted to text a load of her friends, and Lizzy faked a yawn and announced that she would have a shower and another early night.

Their parents left, and Rose sprawled on the sofa with her mobile. But she wasn't concentrating on text messages. Lizzy could almost feel herself being watched every time she turned her back, and at last she said, 'I'm going to have my shower then go to bed. Don't wake me when you come up, OK?'

'Sure,' said Rose carelessly. 'Night.'

Lizzy showered and then went to their shared room. Usually she wore her locket at night. Now, though, she deliberately left it on the table between her own and Rose's bed. Then she settled down under the duvet with a book. She heard Mum and Dad come back, and soon afterwards there was the sound of footsteps on the stairs. Quickly Lizzy switched the light off, and when Rose came in she was pretending to be asleep. There was a pause while Rose's eyes got used to the dark, before the door closed softly and she padded across the room. Lizzy guessed she was standing looking down at her, and resisted an enormous temptation to peek and make sure. Then Rose's bed creaked as she got in, and after that everything was quiet.

Waiting was almost unbearable. Mum and Dad seemed to be taking ages to go to bed tonight, and Lizzy was terrified that she herself might fall asleep. At last, though, the cottage was dark and silent . . . and a short while later Lizzy heard Rose get up. Feet shuffled on the carpet, then there was the tiniest clink from the direction of the bedside table, followed by the sound of someone tiptoeing out of the room.

Lizzy counted to ten before she opened her eyes and sat up. Rose had gone – and so had the locket.

Scrambling out of bed, Lizzy put on her wetsuit,

pulled a jumper and jeans over it and shoved her feet into her most comfortable trainers. Her mobile and a torch went into a small shoulder bag, and, as fast as she could without making a noise, she went downstairs.

There was no sign of Rose, but the back door was unlocked. Lizzy opened it and moved cautiously outside, half afraid that she would run into her sister. She didn't, and after a few seconds she summoned up the courage to hurry to the gate.

The sky was clear and full of stars. Their light was so bright that she could just make out the face of her watch, which read a quarter past twelve. The sea hissed and murmured, white wave crests shining in the starlight as they broke on the rocks, and the air was cool and fresh with a strong salty tang. From the shelter of a tall, straggly bush by the back gate Lizzy peered around, but there was no sign of a hastening figure against the skyline. Which way had Rose gone? Lizzy realized with dismay that she had been too cautious. She should have followed more quickly – Rose could have taken any of several paths, and it was no use trying to guess which the right one was.

Grabbing her mobile from the bag, she called Jack's number. To her relief he answered at once.

'Jack, it's me,' Lizzy said breathlessly, keeping her voice down. 'Rose has gone, and she's taken my locket. She must be on her way to meet Taran – but I've lost her. I don't know which way she went!'

'Don't worry,' said Jack. 'I'm on the launch, and Morvyr and Kes are here too. We can be at the island in a few minutes, and we'll start searching for her. Where are you?'

'Near the cottage.'

'Right. Go to the sandbar where we were this morning. I don't think Rose will meet Taran there, but it's worth checking. Call me if you see her, and I'll do the same.'

He cut the connection, and thankfully Lizzy set off. She didn't dare switch on her torch in case

Rose was nearby and might see it, but the glow from the sky was enough to show her the way. This time she didn't get lost, and soon the dark bulk of the Gugh appeared ahead of her, with the causeway showing like a pale ribbon. At the top of the sandy path she stopped and stared around. There was no one in sight, but the dark shadows of the rocks could easily hide Rose. Lizzy started down the path to the causeway, moving cautiously and crouching low so that her silhouette wouldn't show against the skyline. The sea made a sighing noise as small waves flowed on to the sandbar and drew back again, and the night glow made the water silvery. But there was no sign of Rose.

The muffled shrill of her mobile made her jump, and she grabbed for it, almost dropping it in her hurry to answer. 'Hello?' she whispered eagerly.

'Lizzy, it's me,' said Jack's voice in her ear. 'I think we've found her! Are you at the causeway yet?'

'Yes!' Lizzy's heart seemed to stop beating for a moment then start again much faster.

'Good – wait there, and I'll pick you up.' He rang off.

Not caring now whether anyone saw her, Lizzy ran on down the path to the sandbar. She was halfway across the causeway when she heard the faint sound of an engine. It quickly grew louder, then the dark outline of Jack's motor launch came round the headland, white water churning behind it. Lizzy splashed into the sea and waded to meet it, and Jack helped her to scramble over the gunwale.

'We're not totally sure that it is Rose,' he told her as he turned the boat and headed out to sea again, 'but there's someone with a torch hurrying along a path towards the south side of the island. Kes stayed behind to see where she goes.'

'What about Taran?' Lizzy asked. 'Is there any sign of her?'

Jack shook his head. 'The dolphins are keeping watch but she hasn't made any move yet. Now,

I'm going to stand well off from the shore till we get to the far side, then move in slowly. The last thing we want is for Rose to hear us coming.'

They were both silent as the boat chugged away and turned southwards. Lizzy gazed across the water at the dim, low-lying shapes of the other islands in the distance. Everything was so quiet. No lights showed anywhere and it was hard to believe that in daytime the place was alive with summer visitors. Now, it was like another world. What would the holidaymakers think, she wondered, if they knew of the strange things that were happening here while they slept?

Jack was steering the launch round a jutting spur of rock when Lizzy suddenly grasped his arm. 'Look!' she hissed, pointing.

A torch beam was bobbing along on the crest of the island, crossing a stretch of open, turfy land known as Wingletang Down. Lizzy could just make out the silhouette of a person holding the torch, but from here, and in the darkness, it was impossible to tell whether or not it was Rose.

Jack slowed the launch and the sound of the engine dropped to a gentle burble. Together they watched the hurrying figure, then there was a swirl in the water behind them and Kes surfaced.

'It *is* her,' he said, swimming to the gunwale and hooking his arms over it. 'I went in close and got a good look. There's a fair-sized beach on the south-east side; I think she might be heading there.'

Jack nodded. 'It's a likely place for Taran to choose, if she's coming from further out to sea,' he agreed. 'We'll need to find somewhere to anchor the boat without giving ourselves away. Any ideas, Kes?'

'Yes,' said Kes. 'There's a rock outcrop at this end of the beach. It's high enough to hide the boat behind, and you can look over the top and see what's going on.'

'Great! Then we'd better get ourselves in place before Rose arrives. Lead the way.'

Moving the launch very slowly, so that the engine wouldn't be heard by anyone on shore,

Jack followed Kes further on round the island until a tumble of large rocks appeared ahead. Kes pointed, and the boat nosed quietly into a tiny inlet in the shelter of the outcrop. The sea rose and fell, but it was calm tonight, the waves so small that they were barely breaking. Jack switched off the engine and dropped the anchor over the stern. It caught almost at once, and he tied the painter to a rock spur so that the boat was secure and wouldn't drift. Standing up, he peered cautiously over the rocks, then turned to Lizzy.

'The beach is just on the other side,' he said. 'And I can see Rose's torch. She's coming this way. There's a ledge here, just above the gunwale. If you stand on that you'll be able to watch too. But keep very still. We can't run the risk of being seen.'

Lizzy climbed up beside him and found that the ledge was just high enough to allow her to look over the rocks to the beach beyond. The beach wasn't sandy but was covered with smooth, rounded pebbles, some so big that Lizzy would have needed two hands to pick them up. They looked pale and strange in the starlight, like the landscape of an alien planet. Behind the beach was a shallow bank that led to a grassy path. The small circle of torchlight was bobbing along the path towards them – and a few moments later, Rose's figure showed clearly against the lighter sky.

She was walking steadily and with peculiar confidence, as if she knew every centimetre of the path perfectly. Reaching the bank she jumped down on to the beach, her feet rattling the pebbles as she walked over them. She didn't seem in the least afraid of slipping or slithering; in fact she wasn't even looking where she was going. As if, Lizzy thought, she was in a trance, and another mind was controlling her.

Halfway to the sea's edge Rose stopped and looked around. Lizzy and Jack didn't move a muscle and Lizzy held her breath as well, though Rose couldn't possibly have heard it above the slap and murmur of the sea. After a few seconds Rose seemed satisfied that she was alone, and continued on towards the water. A metre from where the foamy edge of the tide licked she stopped and stood waiting.

A hand touched Jack's leg and, looking down, he saw Kes signalling to him. He and Lizzy lowered themselves back into the boat, and as they sat down the water beyond Kes rippled and Morvyr appeared.

'Jack – Lizzy –' She beckoned them to put their heads down to hers, then whispered in their ears, 'The dolphins have seen Taran!'

Lizzy's heart gave a great thump, and Jack whispered back, 'Where is she?'

'She came through the silver portal, and she's heading this way. She'll be here before long. And she's not wearing the pearl crown!'

Kes's eyes shone with excitement. 'It's what you said would happen, Father – the crown's too precious to risk, so she's left it behind. Which means we can take it from her!'

'And we mustn't waste time,' Morvyr added. 'We must go now.'

Jack took off the locket that hung round his neck and gave it to her. 'Do you remember all that Queen Kara taught you?'

Morvyr smiled at him. 'Oh, yes. I know how to use the pearl.'

'Then . . . good luck.' He looked fondly at the three of them in turn. 'All of you.'

Lizzy had already wriggled free of the clothes she had put on over her wetsuit. She climbed over the launch's gunwale and slid into the water. Morvyr blew Jack a kiss, which he returned. Then without a splash she, Lizzy and Kes slipped under the water and were gone.

Chapter Nine

Morvyr set a fast pace through the dark water, and Lizzy needed all her strength to keep up. The sea felt bitterly cold, and the currents were much trickier than anything she was used to; they criss-crossed and clashed, so that she had to fight to make any progress at all. Again she envied Kes's ability to change from human to merboy. If only she could do the same, could *make* her legs become a tail! She was slowing them down, and because of her they would lose valuable time.

'How – far is the – black pearl's gateway?' she called breathlessly.

Morvyr's voice was carried back to her on the rush of water. 'Not far! But we must hurry – we haven't got long!'

Taran couldn't be far away from the island now. Soon she would arrive at the beach to meet Rose, and then she would discover that she had been tricked . . . Lizzy redoubled her efforts until she felt as if her muscles were tearing.

The moon had risen now, and its silvery light filtered down through the water, brightening the gloom. Suddenly a huge, grey bulk of rock loomed to their left, and Lizzy's eyes widened as Morvyr turned and darted towards it.

'It's all right!' Kes called. 'Mother knows what she's doing!'

Hoping he was right, Lizzy gathered her courage and followed. Then she saw the mouth of a small, narrow cave in the rock. Morvyr swam straight up to the cave, and Lizzy realized that she was going to lead them inside. Beyond the entrance everything was pitch black . . . Lizzy felt a rush of terror, and before she could stop herself she blurted, 'I don't want to go in there!'

Morvyr turned and smiled reassuringly. 'Don't be afraid. This is the gate. And the black pearl will show us the way.'

She opened Jack's locket, then moved her fingers over the secret compartment. It sprang wide, revealing the black pearl, and at once the pearl began to give off a soft, strange glow. Lizzy gazed at it in wonder, for the light itself was almost black too, yet somehow it drove back the darkness. It shone on Morvyr's face and hair, draining them of colour so that she looked like someone in an old photograph. Morvyr smiled.

'Come on,' she said gently.

She swam into the cave. Lizzy and Kes hesitated for a moment. Then they grasped hold of each other's hands and went after her.

The cave was not as deep as Lizzy had feared, and by the glow from the pearl she saw a bowl-shaped hollow in the rocky floor at the back. They gathered round the hollow, and Morvyr held the pearl over it.

A pool of light as eerily colourless as the light of the pearl began to shine in the bowl. Lizzy's memory flashed back to the other gateway, through which she and Kes had travelled when they were forced to take the silver pearl to Taran. She waited, knowing what would come, as the light from the hollow started to move, slowly at first then faster and faster, turning to a whirlpool. Lizzy took a deep breath – then the whirlpool snatched them and spun them and pulled them into the gateway. Twisting and turning, they hurtled down the magical tunnel – then with a rush and a roar their heads broke through water into dazzlingly bright air.

They had surfaced in the pool of the rainbow cave. As the churning water slowly calmed down, Lizzy gazed around. There were the nine mirrors set into the cave walls. Seven shimmered with the colours of the rainbow, the eighth glowed silver. But the ninth was still dark and lifeless, and would stay that way until the black pearl was restored to its place in the Queen's crown. And there was the great rock that Taran used for her throne. It was empty now, but Lizzy remembered the look of cruel triumph on Taran's face as she held up the silver pearl and gloated over her prize.

Morvyr's voice broke the spell of her thoughts. 'Quickly, children!' she said. 'The golden circlet is here somewhere, and we must find it. Look around the rock and the mirrors, and I will swim to the bottom of the pool and search there.'

Without waiting for an answer she dived and vanished. Kes looked at Lizzy. 'Come on,' he said. 'We'd better get started . . .'

Hidden behind the rock outcrop in his gently bobbing boat, Jack waited and watched. There was no sign of Taran yet, and Rose's trancelike mood had begun to wear off. She was growing impatient and now she paced up and down the beach, hands shoved in her pockets, feet scuffing at the pebbles. Even though it was summer the night was chilly as the wind came in off the sea, and every so often Rose shivered and rubbed at her upper arms.

Jack was cold too, but he didn't mind. The longer Taran took to arrive, the happier he would be, because it gave Morvyr and the twins more time for their quest. Where were they now? he wondered. Had they got through the black gateway and reached the rainbow pool? Had they found any trace of the golden circlet? Arhans and the other dolphins might have news, but he had warned them to stay well away from the island in case Taran should see them and become suspicious.

Suddenly a glimmer of silver appeared as something made the sea's surface ripple a short way from the beach. At once Jack was alert, staring over the water. Rose had seen the glimmer too, and she ran to the water's edge, craning eagerly forward. There was another ripple, closer to the shore – then Taran's head and shoulders rose from the water. She was wearing her cloak of seaweed, and bracelets and necklaces made from rare shells hung at her throat and wrists. The moonlight gleamed in her blue-black hair, lit up the emerald green of her eyes. Jack heard Rose gasp at her beauty and he shuddered. Taran was beautiful, all right. Beautiful – and evil.

'Ah, Rose.' The Queen's musical voice carried clearly above the murmur of the sea. 'We meet at last.' Her eyes glinted hungrily. 'Have you brought the black pearl?'

'Yes, Your Majesty.' Rose drew out Lizzy's locket on its chain round her neck, and held it up. 'It's here!'

Taran smiled sweetly. 'Come closer, my dear. Show me.'

Not caring about her jeans or shoes, Rose waded into the sea until the water was above her knees.

'Ahh!' Taran breathed. 'And your sister?'

'She's fast asleep at the cottage we're staying in. She doesn't know anything.'

'Excellent!' Taran swam closer, her gaze never leaving the locket. 'I am sad and disappointed about Lizzy. She was duped by Morvyr, and she really believes that I am a usurper. Poor child; she is very foolish. Such a shame. But then she is so young. You are older. *You* understand the truth.'

'Oh, yes,' said Rose. 'I do. The black pearl is rightfully yours, for you are the true Queen.'

'Of course I am. What a wise girl you are.' Taran smiled her sweetest smile, then reached a hand, palm upwards, towards Rose. 'Now, my dear, give me the pearl.'

'It isn't here!' Lizzy turned from side to side, fists clenched in frustration.

'It must be!' Morvyr had surfaced in the pool and her eyes were frantic.

'Mother, we've looked *everywhere* in the cave,' said Kes. 'There's no sign at all of the circlet! Taran must have hidden it so carefully that we'll never find it!'

'And time's running out,' Lizzy added worriedly.

Morvyr gazed around. 'Oh, where *could* it be?

Unless . . .' Suddenly her expression changed.
'Oh, no . . .'

'What, Mother? What is it?'

'I don't know . . . something . . . a feeling . . .'
A shiver went through Morvyr, and with a flick of
her tail she darted across the pool to where the
black mirror was a dull, dead oval in the cave
wall. Shutting her eyes tightly she added, 'There's
a spell – Queen Kara taught it to me long ago. If
only I can remember it . . . Ah!' Her eyes snapped
open again and she raised the pearl and touched
it to her forehead.

> *'Mirror dark to mirror bright –*
> *Show the truth, and bring the light!'*

To Lizzy's amazement the empty mirror began to
glow with the same strange light that shone from
the black pearl. For several seconds darkness
swirled in its depths. Then, slowly, it cleared, and
a scene appeared. There was the beach on the
island. There was Rose, at the water's edge.

There, too, was Taran. And Rose was holding Lizzy's locket . . .

Rose had trouble with the locket's secret compartment. Taran began to seethe at the delay, and it was all she could do to keep her temper. But at last Rose's fingers found the right spot, and the compartment sprang open.

'The pearl!' Taran hissed. 'Is it there?'

'Yes, Your Majesty.' Carefully, almost reverently, Rose took the fake pearl between finger and thumb and held it up. Jack had painted it very skilfully, laying a silvery sheen over the black so that it looked exactly like the real one.

Taran's sigh of delight sounded like a surging wave. 'Give it to me! *Give it to me!*'

Rose held out the pearl and Taran snatched it. Holding it in her cupped palm she stroked it with greedy fingers. 'I have waited a long time for this moment,' she said, almost crooning in her delight. Then she reached beneath the folds of her seaweed cloak, and drew something out.

Rose said, 'Oh, how lovely!' And Jack peering over the rock felt a surge of horror as he saw what Taran was holding. It was the golden circlet – she had brought it with her after all! So Morvyr and the twins were searching her lair for something that they would never find!

Helplessly Jack watched as Taran raised the circlet in one hand and the pearl in the other. The moon's light seemed to set the circlet on fire, and all the pearls round its edge glowed like brilliant cats' eyes. Then Taran's voice rang out in the night as she chanted the binding spell:

> *'Seven you were; eight you are;*
> *Nine you now shall be.*
> *Let the circle be completed*
> *By the power of moon and sea!*
> *I bind you once, I bind you twice,*
> *And three times with this sign.*
> *The circle is completed –*
> *And now all power is mine!'*

At the same moment that she spoke the last word, Taran touched the black pearl to the last empty setting in the circlet.

Nothing happened. The pearls did not flash their rainbow colours, and the fake black pearl did not magically join with the circlet but simply lay lifeless in Taran's hand.

For a moment Taran was very, very still. Then slowly her head turned and she fixed a terrible stare on Rose. Her eyes seemed to turn to green fire, and her face twisted into a look of towering rage.

'You have tricked me.' Her voice began as a low snarl, then exploded from her in a shrill scream. '*YOU HAVE TRICKED ME!*'

With a powerful thrash of her tail she flung herself forward – and the spell that had hypnotized Rose snapped. Rose jolted awake to see Taran lunging at her. She screamed and tried to scramble back to the shore, but the pebbles under her feet were slippery and treacherous, and with another cry she fell backwards into the water.

'Rose!' Horrified, Jack leaped from the boat and over the rock, scrabbling and slithering in a desperate bid to help. But he was too late. As Rose tried to get to her feet Taran flung the black pearl away and clamped a hand on her arm. The Queen's fingers closed with a grip like an eel's jaws, and she dragged Rose into the sea.

Chapter Ten

'*Rose!*' Lizzy's scream echoed Jack's as the black mirror showed what was happening. She didn't pause, didn't think – spinning on her heel, she dived into the rainbow pool.

She heard Kes and Morvyr yelling at her to come back as she plunged under the water and down, but she ignored their warnings. Rose was in terrible danger, and nothing else mattered! The whirlpool rushed to meet her and she hurled herself into it. It snatched hold of her and carried her away, faster and dizzyingly faster, until she burst out of the gateway in a whirl of bubbles. Gasping, she turned towards the cave entrance and was through it in seconds and swimming with all her strength towards the island. Taran was going to drown Rose – she *had* to be stopped!

Frantically Lizzy churned through the water, arms flailing, feet kicking. Faster, faster, *faster*! But she wasn't fast enough. She didn't have the power, didn't have the speed!

Suddenly a shock went through her, a violent tingling that seemed to start in her head and surge down to her feet. Her feet – they *weren't* feet any more! She was changing – she could feel it – her legs fusing together, her feet becoming one, becoming a tail. *She was a mermaid!*

Lizzy gave a strange, wild cry of triumph and hope as, swift as a dolphin, she hurtled towards the place where Rose was fighting for her life.

It took Jack only a few seconds to start the engine, but even as he powered the launch out of the rocks' shelter and into open sea, he knew that there was nothing he could do. Taran and Rose had vanished beneath the surface; he could pinpoint the spot where they had gone under, but he wouldn't be able to reach them without diving over the side. He couldn't breathe water – he couldn't help Rose!

'Arhans!' he roared. '*Arhans, help us, quickly!*' But the dolphins might be anywhere. Even if Arhans had heard him, she was probably too far away to get here in time.

Then, further out to sea, he saw water splash and churn, and for a moment the flukes of a shining tail appeared above the surface. For a moment he thought it was a dolphin. Then he realized how wrong he was.

Through a dark whirl of water Lizzy saw Rose and Taran ahead of her. Rose was struggling, but her struggles were becoming weaker and Taran's grip was relentless. She was pulling Rose down, deeper into the sea, and a surge of mixed fury and desperation went through Lizzy and gave her new energy. Bunching her fists and stretching both arms ahead of her, she put on a final burst of speed and charged straight at the evil Queen.

Taran's back was to Lizzy and she didn't see her coming. Lizzy hit her full on, and the impact sent Taran spinning sideways. She lost her hold on Rose, who at once started to sink. Darting frantically after her, Lizzy grabbed her under both arms and surged towards the surface. But Rose was a limp weight; she had lost consciousness and her sodden clothes were dragging her down. Even if Lizzy could reach the surface with her, could she get her to shore?

In the chaos of the moment she had not heard the noise of an approaching engine. But as she and Rose came up into the moonlit air, she saw the launch heading fast towards them with Jack at the wheel.

Lizzy waved frantically, spluttering as air and water mingled in her mouth. She almost let go of Rose but just managed to grab her again, then Jack was there, stopping the boat and leaning over to take the heavy burden.

'I've got her!' He heaved Rose over the gunwale, then as she fell into the launch his eyes widened with alarm and he shouted, 'Lizzy, look out!'

Lizzy turned just in time to see Taran speeding towards her. The Queen's face was ugly with rage and her hands were outstretched like claws. There was no time for anything but instinct and, as Taran lunged to attack, Lizzy's tail flipped and she dived. Taran shot past above her, then while Lizzy righted herself the Queen twisted with incredible agility and came at her again. An arm lashed out and Lizzy dodged, her tail swishing round and slapping across Taran's midriff. Then through the foaming and bubbling of the water she saw a flash of gold. The circlet! A reckless impulse hit her like a lightning strike. If she could get hold of it –

She didn't pause to think but hurled herself at Taran. Taken by surprise, the Queen was thrown off balance, and Lizzy's fingers clamped on the circlet. The two of them struggled ferociously as she tried to pull the circlet from the Queen's grasp, but Taran was much bigger and stronger, and Lizzy began to lose her grip. She made a last, despairing effort to wrest it away – and suddenly she somersaulted backwards as Taran gave a scream and let go.

The long pole of a boathook had speared down from above them and caught in Taran's seaweed cloak. *Jack!* Lizzy realized with delight. He must have glimpsed them under the water, and he was helping her! Jack pulled on the pole, jerking Taran away. She tried to free herself but her arms and tail were tangled in the cloak's folds.

Lizzy took her chance. Turning, she darted away with the circlet in her hand. She heard Taran scream at her to come back, but she did not pause. She had to reach the rainbow pool and find Kes and Morvyr, so that the black pearl could be restored and the circlet made whole again!

Suddenly Taran's cries changed from fury to triumph. Lizzy flung a glance over her shoulder, and saw that the Queen had torn herself free from the cloak and was giving chase. Horrified,

Lizzy thrashed her tail with all the energy she could summon. She had a head start and she was swimming as fast as she could – but Taran was faster. Slowly but surely she began to catch up, until Lizzy knew with an awful certainty that she was going to be overtaken. Had Jack seen what had happened? Was he following? Could he do anything? And Kes and Morvyr, and the dolphins – where *were* they all?

'Arhans! Mother!' She could hardly spare breath for shouting, but she was desperate. 'Help me, oh, please help!'

Taran was no more than ten metres behind her now, and closing. Fear gave Lizzy extra power and she put on a burst of speed. But it wasn't going to be enough.

Suddenly from somewhere ahead a voice called, 'Lizzy!' and Kes and Morvyr emerged from the gloomy dimness. They were riding on the backs of two dolphins, and the others were there too, with Arhans leading them.

'Lizzy, the circlet!' cried Morvyr. 'Give it to me

quickly!' She slid off her dolphin's back and raced towards Lizzy. Fumbling in her haste Lizzy dropped the circlet, but Morvyr dived after it as it began to sink. Her hand closed round it, and with her other hand she touched the black pearl to its rim.

The eight pearls set in the circlet began to glow. Taran saw it and swirled to a halt.

'No,' she snarled, glaring at Morvyr. 'Oh, no. You won't *dare*!'

'Won't I?' Morvyr smiled icily. Then her voice called clearly over the surge and rumble of the tide:

'Seven you were; eight you are;
Nine you now shall be.
Let the circle be completed
By the power of moon and sea!'

A quivering rainbow of light sprang outwards from Morvyr's hands, and Taran's eyes widened with alarm. She raised her arms, summoning her

power, but before she could muster her spell
Morvyr called again:

> *'Three times three I bind you*
> *Within the crown of light.*
> *The circle now is whole again,*
> *And evil put to flight!'*

As Morvyr uttered the final word, the rainbow
light flared outwards. It flowed over Lizzy
and Kes, bathing them in fantastic haloes of
colour. Then it seemed to gather itself into a
single dazzling beam, and a charge of glittering
energy seared through the sea and struck Taran
full on.

The evil Queen screamed and went tumbling
backwards, twisting over and over. The beam of
energy vanished as Taran struggled to regain her
balance, and for a second or two she stared at
Morvyr and the twins. Her face was blank with
shock, her mouth gaped open as if she could not
believe what had happened. Then she gave a wail

of despair, turned with a violent thrash of her tail and fled.

Morvyr looked at Arhans and said, 'Stop her!'

Arhans whistled a high-pitched command, and the five dolphins peeled off to the right and left and streaked after Taran. As they vanished in the darkness, Morvyr turned to Lizzy and Kes. She still held the circlet, and Lizzy saw that it was no longer mere dull gold, but glowed and shimmered and sparkled as though it had an inner light of its own.

'It's done,' Morvyr said softly. 'At last, Taran's power is broken.' Reaching out, she hugged Lizzy to her. 'You saved the crown, Lizzy – you saved us all!' Then she drew back and smiled as she gazed at Lizzy's tail. 'And found yourself at the same time.'

Chapter Eleven

Lizzy's lower lip started to tremble. 'It was for Rose,' she whispered. 'Taran was going to drown her. So I just . . . just . . .' The words broke off in a stifled sob.

'You were brilliant, Lizzy,' said Kes. He, too, put an arm round her, then gave a teasing tug at her hair. 'You're *really* a mermaid now!'

The water above them churned, and they all heard the sound of an engine.

'It's Father!' Eagerly Kes let go of Lizzy and swam towards the surface. Taking Lizzy's hand, Morvyr followed, and when their heads came up above the water they saw Kes, with Jack in the launch beside him.

'Rose!' Letting go of Morvyr's hand Lizzy swam to the boat. 'Is she all right?'

'She'll be fine,' Jack reassured her. 'She swallowed a bit of sea water, but I got that out of her and she's starting to recover now.'

Hooking her arms over the gunwale, Lizzy heaved herself up and looked over the side. Rose was lying in the launch, with Jack's coat and sweater round her shoulders. Her eyes were open, though she looked a little dazed, and when she saw Lizzy staring anxiously at her she managed a shaky grin.

'I'm OK,' she said. 'Though I very nearly wasn't. Thanks, sis.'

Lizzy felt her face turning scarlet, and to cover it she said, 'We've got to get you back to shore, before you get pneumonia.'

'Oh, don't be a muppet. I'm fine!' Rose struggled to sit up and Jack helped her. She coughed, wiped her mouth, then added in something more like her usual, Rose-ish way, 'And if you think I'm going to just go home and miss out *now*, you've got another think coming!' Morvyr had reached the boat by this time, and Rose looked expectantly at them all in turn. 'So come on, tell me, what's happened?'

Morvyr smiled at her, and held up the golden circlet.

'Wow . . .' Rose breathed. Jack, too, stared at the circlet, then let out a long, soft sigh.

'You did it.' There was admiration in his voice.

'*Lizzy* did it,' said Morvyr. 'She unlocked the power of her own nature to help Rose when she was in danger. And that gave her the strength to outwit Taran.'

Kes grinned broadly. 'She makes a great mermaid, Father, don't you think?' he said. 'And you should have seen how fast she swam when Taran was chasing her! Before we know it, she'll be a better swimmer than me!'

'She's a terrific mermaid,' Jack agreed, leaning

over to ruffle Lizzy's wet hair. 'And I'm very, very proud of her.'

Lizzy felt tears welling, and fiercely told herself to stop being silly. Everything had come out right – Rose was safe, Taran was defeated and the crown had been restored to its full glory and power. Whatever was there to *cry* about?

Jack understood, though. He would have said something, but before he could a shrill whistling sounded from somewhere in the distance.

'It's the dolphins,' said Morvyr. She looked out across the moonlit sea. 'They're coming back.' She peered harder. 'And there's someone else with them.'

The dolphins were heading towards them in close formation. First came Arhans, then behind her two of the others, who seemed to be towing something, while the fourth and fifth dolphins swam alongside like guards. They drew nearer, until the mysterious shape was recognizable.

It was Taran. Her arms and tail were tightly bound, and she was being pulled helplessly along by long seaweed ropes, which the second and third dolphins held in their mouths. Excited chittering noises rang across the water as the dolphins announced their arrival, and Arhans rushed up to the boat, slapping her tail jubilantly on the water and splashing everyone as she stopped. More whistling and chattering followed, and Morvyr translated for Lizzy.

'Arhans says it was a hard chase, but they were too fast for Taran,' she told her. Then her mouth curved in a smile. 'She tried to use magic against them. But it didn't work. Her power really *is* gone.'

Lizzy and Kes laughed delightedly, and Taran snarled at them in a way that reminded Lizzy of Tullor.

'Thieves!' she spat. 'Traitors and thieves!'

'*You* are the traitor and thief, Taran, not us,' Morvyr replied coldly. 'But your reign is over, and you'll never hold power in the undersea world again.'

'What shall we do with her?' Jack asked.

'There's only one person who can decide,' said

Morvyr. 'The *true* Queen will choose her fate.'

'Ha!' Taran retorted. 'There is no true Queen – she died years ago!' Her face grew ugly and she added with a sneer, '*I* saw to that!'

Morvyr gave her a look of utter contempt. 'Yes, you murdered Queen Kara. But Karwynna, her daughter and heir, is alive. I know, because I heard you talking to Tullor in the cave of the rainbow pool.'

Taran was clearly shocked, but she quickly hid it and sneered again. 'Oh, you are *very* clever! All right, so Karwynna is still alive. But do you know where she is?' Morvyr's face showed dismay before she could hide it, and Taran laughed harshly. 'I thought not!'

'We'll find her,' said Morvyr angrily.

'Will you? How loyal you are! And where will you start? She could be anywhere in the world. How long will it take you to search the whole world, Morvyr?' She laughed again. 'You'll all die of old age before you discover her hiding place!'

Up till now Jack had said nothing, but suddenly
he couldn't keep silent any longer. 'Tell us where
she is!' he demanded furiously. 'Tell us, Taran, or
I'll –'

'No.' Morvyr stopped him. 'Don't threaten her,
Jack. That's *her* way of treating people, and we're
not like her.' She looked at Taran again and her
eyes were the colour of a storm cloud. 'Will you
tell us where Karwynna is?'

Taran tossed her head so that her black hair
flew around her shoulders. 'What sort of fool do
you take me for? Find her yourself – if you can!'

'You've lost the crown and your power. You
can't gain anything by refusing to tell us.'

'Oh, but I can. I'll have the pleasure of knowing
you'll never see Karwynna alive again.'

Morvyr sighed and turned back to her
companions. 'It's no use. Even now, she's so full
of spite and hatred that she won't admit she's
beaten. There's no point trying any more, and we
have more important things to do than argue with
her. Arhans – Taran is your prisoner now. Take

her to a safe place, and set guards over her to make sure she can't escape.'

Arhans whistled agreement, and no one spoke while Taran's bindings were checked and tightened. As Lizzy watched, a thought began to nag at the back of her mind. Something Taran had said: *She could be anywhere in the world.* It was important in some way. But how? She couldn't work it out.

Taran didn't make any protest. In fact when the dolphins took hold of the seaweed ropes and bore her away, she was smiling.

'Well,' Morvyr said despondently when the defeated Queen and her escort had vanished into the darkness, 'we *must* begin the search for Karwynna. But Taran was right: even with the help of all our friends, how long *will* it take us to search the whole world?'

And the thing that had been bothering Lizzy suddenly slotted into place.

She said in a voice that wasn't quite steady, 'Eleven years . . .'

'What?' Kes, Morvyr and Jack all stared at her. Kes and Morvyr looked baffled – but Jack understood.

'Yes,' he said softly. 'Oh, yes . . . it's the same game that she played before! Lizzy, you're a genius!'

'Is she?' Kes demanded. 'Why? What do you two know that we don't?'

'When Lizzy was kidnapped all those years ago,' Jack said, 'we were led to believe that she'd been taken far away. So I went on a wild-goose chase to look for her. But all the time she was hidden right under our noses!'

Kes's jaw dropped. 'Oh! You mean Taran's trying that trick again? Then we haven't got to search the world to find Karwynna. She's somewhere *here*!'

For a second or two there was silence but for the hiss of the sea on the rocks. Then Morvyr looked at the golden circlet in her hands and said quietly, 'Yes. And I think I know where.' There was a new light in her eyes as she turned to the twins. 'I'm going back to the rainbow cave. Do you want to come with me?'

Their eager faces gave her the answer before they chorused, 'Yes!'

'You're not too tired?'

'*No!*'

Jack laughed. 'They'd go even if they were dropping from exhaustion,' he said. 'As for me, though, I'd better take Rose back to the cottage, and make sure she gets safely inside.'

'But I'm missing all the excitement!' Rose said plaintively.

Jack was sympathetic. 'I know it doesn't seem fair, Rose. But there won't be anything exciting to see here for a while. And you and I can't go under the sea with Morvyr and the twins,' he added wistfully.

Rose sighed. 'I suppose not.' Then she glared fiercely at Lizzy. 'But the *moment* you get back, I want to know all about it, OK?'

Lizzy returned the glare with a broad grin. 'You bet!'

Morvyr blew a kiss to Jack. And moments later there was only the slowly moving sea where she, Lizzy and Kes had been.

Chapter Twelve

The moon was setting, and the undersea world dim and mysterious, but Morvyr headed unerringly towards the black pearl's gateway. Lizzy and Kes swam beside her. Lizzy was keyed up and nervous, and very tired now, though she didn't want to admit it. Yet all those things were eclipsed by a sense of wonder at the thought of all they had done. Taran was defeated and would never trouble the sea people again. And she herself had found her long-lost family and learned at last to become a mermaid. It was almost too much to believe. But as she glided through the water, feeling the strength of her tail powering her along, Lizzy knew that her incredible dream had come true.

It was so dark that the great rock with its narrow cave was almost invisible until they were nearly on top of it. Again Lizzy felt a stab of fear as Morvyr led the way through the cave entrance and into the pitch-black tunnel beyond. They reached the pool, and Morvyr held the golden circlet over it. The black pearl started to glow; light answered from within the pool, and with a rush and roar and swirl they were pulled into the gateway.

They surfaced together in the rainbow pool, surrounded by the mirrors in the cave wall. The first thing that struck Lizzy was the silence after the roar of the sea outside. It was crazy, because this place was always quiet. But somehow it seemed more so now. Instinctively she looked towards the rock that Taran had used as her throne, half expecting to see the evil Queen staring haughtily down with her cold green eyes. But Taran was gone for good, and there was a sense of peace in the cave that she had never felt before.

Kes, too, was gazing around, and when he spoke his voice was hushed as if he didn't want to spoil the quiet atmosphere.

'Is . . . is Karwynna here, Mother?'

'I think she is.' Morvyr swam to the centre of the pool, then raised the golden circlet above her head. Slowly and carefully she turned it, until each pearl pointed to its matching mirror. When they were all lined up, the pearls began to glow – and the mirrors answered. Their surfaces swirled. Slowly but steadily they brightened until the cave was filled with light, shimmering in every colour of the rainbow.

Lizzy and Kes gasped with delight, and Morvyr said, 'This is how the cave used to look when Kara was Queen and her crown was whole.'

'It's beautiful!' Lizzy breathed.

'Yes. And it's a symbol of the Queen's power.'

'But where *is* the real Queen?' Kes asked. 'There's no sign of her.'

'Then we must call to her,' said Morvyr. 'Children, do you remember the rhyme that Jack recited to you? The one that was written after Taran seized power?'

'Yes,' said Lizzy. 'He said it was to remind the sea people that Taran's rule couldn't last forever. I learned it, and I told it to Kes.'

Morvyr smiled. 'Good. Then place your hands on the crown, and say the rhyme with me now.'

She lowered the circlet so that the twins could reach it. Lizzy and Kes looked at each other and drew deep, nervous breaths. Then, very carefully, they laid their hands on the circlet. It felt strangely warm, and the glow from the nine pearls spilled between their fingers and stained them with colour.

Together, all three of them began to repeat the rhyme:

'Red is the sunrise, Orange the sky,
Golden the shimmering sand.
Green are the pools where the small fishes lie,

Blue water rolls to the land.
Indigo shadows hide secrets in caves,
Violet the glow of the night.
But Silver and Black will call them all back
When a terrible wrong is put right.'

The last words faded away and for the space of two heartbeats the cave was silent again. Then, shockingly and unexpectedly, there was a deafening *CRACK*. The mirrors shook, the rainbow lights danced wildly – and Taran's throne shattered apart. Chunks of broken rock tumbled from the ledge and splashed into the pool, some narrowly missing Morvyr and the twins, and the water churned and heaved so that they were almost swamped.

The rocks sank and the pool calmed down. Spluttering, shaking water from her face, Lizzy looked back at the ledge – and her eyes widened.

The throne was nothing but rubble. The rock had split and broken open, revealing the fact that it was hollow. Inside lay a mermaid.

She was younger than Taran, and much more

beautiful. Her hair was like a sapphire-blue waterfall, cascading to her waist and framing a delicate face with a faint silvery tinge to the skin. Her tail was bright turquoise, with silver scales that glittered like sequins. Her eyes were closed, and she seemed to be fast asleep.

'Mother!' Kes could only stare and stare at the mermaid. 'Is it –' He swallowed, too afraid to ask the question in case he was wrong.

But there was joy on Morvyr's face. 'Yes,' she said. 'It's Karwynna!'

With a powerful flip of her own tail she swam across the pool to the broken rock. 'Karwynna! Queen Karwynna! We've come to rescue you!'

The mermaid did not move, and Lizzy looked at Morvyr in alarm. 'She's not . . . *dead*?'

'No,' said Morvyr. 'I think she's in a trance. Taran must have cast a spell on her, and she won't wake up unless we can break it.'

'But how? Do you know?'

Morvyr hesitated. 'I'm not sure,' she said at last. 'But the crown helped us to find her, and now I think it will help us again. We must place it on her head. She's the true Queen, and I believe the crown has the power to break the spell.' She looked to right and left, studying the ledge. 'How can I climb up? The side is sheer, and I don't have the magic that Taran used . . .' Abruptly she turned to the twins. 'But *you* can do it. If you change to human shape, you can both climb it easily.'

Kes said eagerly, 'Yes, of course!' But Lizzy hesitated, suddenly afraid. *Could* she change back to her human form simply by willing it to happen? What if she couldn't make it work again? And, even if she did, would she be able to become a mermaid once more, or would her new-found ability desert her?

Kes saw the doubt on her face and understood. 'You *can* do it, Lizzy!' he urged. 'Once a mermaid, always a mermaid – come on, just try!'

Lizzy looked nervously from Kes to Morvyr. Then she closed her eyes and thought: *I'm human. I'm human . . .*

'Oh!' Her eyes snapped open and her mouth opened too as a tingling sensation went through her tail. She tried to move it, but suddenly she seemed to have two tails instead of one. Or – no, they weren't tails, they were legs! And her fins had become feet, with toes that she could flex and wiggle.

Kes burst out laughing. 'Your face!' he said. 'You look so surprised!'

Fully restored to human shape, Lizzy glowered at him, then she saw the funny side and laughed too.

'Lizzy, Kes!' Morvyr tried to sound stern but her own mouth was twitching. 'This is no time for games! You have a solemn task to do.'

The twins sobered, though Kes still had to stifle an occasional giggle. He, too, had changed his shape, and together they scrambled up to the rock ledge and stood gazing down at Karwynna.

'She's so still,' Lizzy said uneasily.

Kes nodded. 'But she's breathing. Look.'

Morvyr, still in the pool, stretched out her

141

arms, the circlet grasped in her hands. 'Take it, children, and give it to its rightful owner.'

Very carefully Kes reached down and took the circlet from her. He carried it to where Karwynna lay . . . then, to Lizzy's surprise, he stopped and held it out to her.

'You do it, Lizzy,' he said. 'Without you, none of this would have happened. So you should be the one to give the Queen her crown.'

A choking sensation clutched at Lizzy's chest. 'No,' she whispered. 'I don't deserve it . . .'

But Morvyr said, 'Kes is right, Lizzy. The honour is yours. You've earned it.'

Lizzy was outnumbered and couldn't argue. With shaking hands she accepted the circlet and moved to stand beside Karwynna. The circlet seemed to tug at her fingers, as though it was eager to be returned to its true place. Slowly and reverently Lizzy lowered it until it touched Karwynna's hair and settled there. It fitted perfectly. And as Lizzy's hands drew back, the silver and black pearls began to sing in soft harmony, while the other seven pearls pulsed with their rainbow colours.

A sigh came from the sleeping mermaid's throat. Then her eyelids flickered, and Lizzy and Kes found themselves gazing into a pair of exquisite, silver-flecked turquoise eyes.

Karwynna blinked. 'I was dreaming . . .' she murmured, and then her vision seemed to focus and she saw the eager faces of Lizzy and Kes gazing down at her. In a puzzled voice she asked, 'Who are you . . .?'

'They are my children, Your Majesty,' said Morvyr from the pool. 'And thanks to them, you can now claim your rightful place as our Queen.'

Chapter Thirteen

Jack took Rose to the holiday cottage and tried to persuade her to stay there, but Rose was having none of that. She was perfectly all right, she said. All she needed was to change into dry clothes and leave a note for Mr and Mrs Baxter saying that she and Lizzy had gone for an early walk.

'They won't wake up for hours yet, anyway,' she added. 'And I've missed so much of the excitement. I'm not going to miss any more – I'm staying with you till Lizzy and the others come back!'

Jack gave way. They returned to the little cove,

and now the two of them were sitting together on the pebble beach. Time was passing. The moon had disappeared completely now, and soon the first faint glimmer of dawn would lighten the sky behind them. The early morning air was chilly, but Rose took no notice as she stared out over the sea, anxiously scanning for any sign of the returning party. Every fifteen seconds the double flash of the Bishop Rock lighthouse, four miles out to the south-west, swept across the sky and dimmed the stars. She must have counted nearly a hundred flashes but still Lizzy and the others had not come back.

'Do you think everything's all right?' Rose asked after a while. 'If Lizzy was wrong, and they can't find Karwynna −'

'We'll just have to wait and see,' said Jack. 'But I think Lizzy was right.' He smiled. 'She's a clever girl, your sister.'

Rose nodded, then frowned. 'It's a bit weird to think that she isn't my sister at all. I mean, I know she isn't really, because we're both adopted, but I've always *thought* of us as sisters. Now, though . . .' Her voice tailed off helplessly. 'I don't know what to think about anything.'

'If I were you,' said Jack, 'I wouldn't. Think about it, I mean. Lizzy's still Lizzy, even if she can live underwater like Kes and Morvyr.'

'Ye-es. But that's just it, isn't it? What's going to happen to her now? Can she still be happy living on land with us, or – or –'

'Will she want to go back to the sea?' Jack sighed. 'I don't know, Rose. I truly don't. And I don't suppose Lizzy does, either.'

Rose nodded again, biting her lower lip. Then her next question came in a rush. 'What do *you* want her to do?'

Jack had been thinking a lot about that, and had decided that there was only one answer that was fair. 'I want her to make her own choice,' he said. 'Whatever it is.'

Rose considered that for a moment or two, then gave an odd little laugh. 'I sort of thought you'd say that. You're putting Lizzy first, of course.

I wish I could be as generous as you, but I can't. You see, I – I don't want to lose her.'

Jack was about to say firmly that in his opinion there was no chance of that, when abruptly Rose tensed. 'Look!' she said, pointing at the sea. 'Out there!' She scrambled to her feet, slithering on the pebbles. 'It's the dolphins!'

Five curved fins had broken the surface, and as Jack, too, got to his feet, Arhans and her friends burst from under the water and leaped joyfully into the air, whistling shrilly. Then three heads, two blonde and one dark, surfaced behind them.

Rose let out a joyful shriek. '*Lizzy!*' She ran into the sea, with Jack right behind her, until the small waves were surging round their knees. Lizzy waved wildly, and as she swam towards the beach they heard her calling, 'We've found her! We've found her! She's alive!'

She splashed to Rose and hugged her, almost dancing in the shallows. Kes hurried after her, and Morvyr swam as close as she could, her eyes shining. For a while there was complete confusion as Lizzy and Kes breathlessly babbled disjointed bits of their story while Rose bombarded them with questions. At last, though, everyone calmed down a little. And then, her voice almost shaking with excitement, Lizzy said, 'And there's something else! Something amazing – an invitation –' She turned to Morvyr. 'Mother, you tell them!'

Morvyr smiled dazzlingly. 'Jack – Rose – Tomorrow night, Queen Karwynna is to call a gathering of her loyal friends. And she especially wants you both to be there.'

Rose stared at her, wide-eyed. '*Me?*' she said incredulously. 'Why me? Jack, of course; that's only right! But I haven't done anything to help Queen Karwynna.' Her face became unhappy. 'I did the opposite. I almost wrecked everything!'

'You didn't, Rose,' said Jack. 'If it hadn't been for you, Taran wouldn't have been lured from her lair, and we couldn't have defeated her.'

'Anyway,' Lizzy added loyally, 'Taran hypnotized you. You didn't *want* to help her. You wanted to help us, and you did!'

'That's right,' said Kes, grinning. 'You were the bait, and Taran snapped it up!'

Rose looked from one to another of them, bewildered and confused and not knowing what to say. But they were all smiling at her now, and Jack said, 'Well, Rose? Will you come and meet the new Queen tomorrow?'

Rose hesitated, but only for a moment before her face lit up with joy. 'Oh, yes, please!'

How she and Rose got through the day Lizzy would never know. The strain of pretending everything was normal, so as not to arouse Mr and Mrs Baxter's suspicions, was almost unbearable. But at last the day was over, and as soon as they were sure Mum and Dad were asleep, the two girls tiptoed out of the holiday cottage and set off for the pebble cove.

As they hurried over the springy turf of the down Lizzy wanted to tell Rose how happy she was that they were really sharing this adventure at last, but she couldn't find the words. So instead she caught hold of her sister's hand and squeezed it. Rose didn't say anything either, but she looked at Lizzy and smiled, and Lizzy knew she understood.

Jack had brought the motor launch to the cove, and with him were Morvyr, Kes and Arhans. There was a happy smile on Jack's face, with something almost enigmatic about it, as though he had some special secret. Lizzy was curious, but everyone else was anxious to be away and there was no time to ask questions. The girls climbed into the boat, and they chugged steadily out to sea with the others swimming beside them.

The towering lighthouse seemed to grow bigger as they headed towards it, and soon the beam was strong enough to light their faces as it swept by.

'Where are we going?' Lizzy asked, raising her voice above the noise of the engine and the sea and the wind.

'Not much further,' said Jack. 'See that tiny island, between us and the lighthouse? That's about the right place.'

'But it's just a rock – there's nothing there.' She was mystified.

Jack's enigmatic smile came back. 'Ah, but there is,' he said. 'You'll see when we get there.'

The boat motored on. The island Jack had pointed out came closer and closer – then suddenly Rose grabbed Lizzy's arm and cried, 'Look! Oh, look!'

The great lighthouse beam was sweeping round again, and as it lit up the sea around the boat, they saw shapes in the water, leaping and surging and gliding effortlessly along with them.

'Dolphins and seals!' Rose was almost bouncing with delight. 'Oh, how *amazing*!'

'They've come to welcome Queen Karwynna too!' Morvyr called. 'They're all so happy that Taran has gone!'

They were nearly at the little island now, and the boat slowed down as Jack throttled back the engine. More dolphins and seals were coming from every direction and gathering around the rocks. The water seemed to be alive with swimming creatures, and the noise of the dolphins' whistling was like strange sea music.

Jack turned to Rose and Lizzy and smiled. 'This,' he said, 'is where we get out and swim!'

'*What?*' Rose's jaw dropped. 'What do you mean?'

'This island is very close to the black pearl's gateway,' Jack told her. 'And that's where we're going – through the gateway to the rainbow pool. All of us.'

Rose was horrified. 'Under the sea? I can't do that! I won't be able to breathe!'

'You will, Rose. We both will.' Jack took something from his pocket. 'Morvyr gave me these while we were waiting for you. They're a very special gift from the new Queen.'

Clasped in his hand were two closed oyster shells. Rose stared uncertainly at them. 'What are they? I don't understand.'

Morvyr had swum to the side of the boat. 'Queen Karwynna learned the magic from her mother long ago,' she said. 'The shells contain a potion that will allow you and Jack to breathe under the sea, just as we can do. The effect will last long enough for you to visit Queen Karwynna in her court.'

Rose's eyes opened wide with amazement. She tried to say something but she was speechless.

Lizzy wasn't, though. 'Oh, Jack, this is wonderful!' Eyes shining, she turned to Rose. 'You'll come, won't you?' she begged. 'Please say you will!'

'There's no danger,' Jack added, seeing that Rose didn't know whether to be thrilled or terrified. 'We'll all look after you. It's a once-in-a-lifetime chance.'

'Yes,' Rose whispered. 'Yes, it is, isn't it?' She hesitated, then: 'I'll come!'

Lizzy hugged her joyfully, and Kes punched the air in delighted triumph and turned a somersault in the water.

Jack gave Rose one of the oyster shells. 'Open it very carefully − like this.' He laid the other shell in the palm of one hand, and with the other gently prised the two halves open. Inside was a tiny pool of liquid that sparkled with all the colours of the rainbow. Rose, still wide-eyed, opened her own shell and gazed in wonder.

'All you have to do is drink it,' said Jack. He smiled. 'Shall we both do it together?'

She nodded. They put their shells to their lips and drank. Rose swallowed, blinked, and sat very still, as if she was waiting for something to happen. After a few seconds she said, 'I don't feel any different . . .'

'Oh, you will,' Jack assured her. 'Come on. I'll hold one of your hands and Lizzy will hold the other. Ready?'

'W-what about the boat?' At the last moment Rose looked frantically for an excuse. 'If we're not here, it'll drift away . . .'

'The dolphins will make sure it doesn't.'

It was now or never. Rose looked frantically at Lizzy, but Lizzy only smiled and held out her hand. Rose gripped it as hard as she could . . . and the three of them plunged into the sea and dived downwards.

Chapter Fourteen

At first Rose was too stunned to say anything as they swam towards the black pearl gateway, but Lizzy knew exactly how she must be feeling. She remembered the first time she herself had discovered that she could breathe under the sea; first the fear and bewilderment, then slowly growing confidence as the fear faded and was replaced by wonder. It was just the same for Rose, and once the early terror was gone, she was thrilled and awed by what was happening to her.

Lizzy could now change her shape simply by willing it to happen, and when she turned into a mermaid Rose gave a cry of delight.

'I don't *believe* it!' she said, and batted, laughing, at the bubbles that streamed from her mouth when she spoke. 'People talk about swimming with dolphins – but I'm swimming with mermaids, as well! It's – it's just so *incredible*!'

She was between Lizzy and Kes, arms linked with theirs as they followed Jack and Morvyr, who were clasping each other's hands. Jack seemed completely at home in the water. Now and then he looked back at the others and Lizzy saw a smile of joy on his face. They had left the dolphins and seals behind, but here in the depths other creatures had gathered too. Fish of every size and kind darted, their scales shining in the dimness. Octopus and squid propelled themselves along, their tentacles waving, followed by a group of blue jellyfish like exotic living jewels. Enchanted, Rose gazed and gazed, trying to take in everything at once.

Soon the cave mouth appeared below them, and they swam through and into the narrow tunnel to the gateway. Light was already glowing in the portal, and as they approached it a lovely voice, quite unlike Taran's, spoke from the gateway's depths and said, 'Welcome!'

Rose didn't know what to expect, and Lizzy heard her scream as they were whirled and tumbled through the gate. She shouted, 'It's all right, don't be frightened!' but almost before the words were out, the wild ride ended and they surfaced in the pool of the rainbow cave.

Lizzy gasped aloud – for the cave was transformed. All nine mirrors were shining brilliantly, the coloured light mingling and dancing and sparkling over the roof and walls. All around the ledge at the edge of the pool sat the new Queen's own people – the merfolk. Old and young, men and women and children, with flowing hair and tails of a dozen different shimmering colours. Some wore cloaks of seaweed, others necklaces and bracelets made from shells of every kind, and some even had sea anemones clinging to their hair like living flowers. They were smiling down at the five newcomers.

And on a throne fashioned from two giant scallop shells and wonderfully decorated with anemones and corals and jewel-coloured seaweed, sat Queen Karwynna herself.

She looked even more beautiful than when she had first woken from her magical trance. Her hair and tail shone with all the colours of a sunlit sea, and there was wisdom and kindness and merriment in her turquoise eyes. The golden circlet, now complete with its nine pearls, was set on her head, and in one hand she held a slender sceptre made from mother-of-pearl and carved with the emblem of a leaping dolphin.

Karwynna, too, smiled down, and in a voice that was gentle and powerful and musical said, 'Thank you, Morvyr, for bringing your children to me! And Jack – I was very young when we last met, but I remember you well.' Then her gaze focused on the last of the five. 'And this is Rose?'

Rose was shaking so much that Lizzy and Kes had to hang on to her arms to keep her afloat. 'Y-yes, Your M-m-majesty . . .' she managed to stammer.

'Thank you, my dear, for what you did to help me,' said Karwynna. 'You are a hundred times welcome.'

Rose was nearly in tears. 'But I didn't help you,' she said miserably. 'I almost r-ruined everything . . .'

'Hush!' Karwynna put a finger to her own lips. 'Without you, this happy moment could not have come to be.' A hint of mischief showed in her eyes. 'Isn't that a good enough reason for us to be friends?' She leaned down and held out a hand. 'Come and sit beside me, and then I can get to know you better.'

Within another minute they were all sitting on the ledge with the merfolk crowding round them. Many of them knew Jack from years ago and were thrilled to see him and Lizzy and hear their stories. Lizzy, in her turn, was enthralled to discover that many of the merfolk were her own aunts and uncles and cousins. Even Rose got over her first shyness and was soon joining in with the rest. The cave echoed with talk and laughter until

Karwynna suddenly said, 'My friends, this is a wonderful occasion for us all – but we still have a serious matter to deal with.' She turned to three of the older merfolk, two men and a woman. 'I think it's time to deal with our prisoner.'

The three bowed, slipped into the pool and vanished under the water, and Rose looked at Lizzy and whispered uneasily, 'She means Taran . . . Oh, Lizzy, what's she going to do when she sees me?'

'Nothing!' Lizzy whispered back, her voice fierce. 'There's nothing she *can* do, not any more!'

Everyone was a little quiet until the three merfolk came back – and with them was a fourth.

They had taken no chances with Taran. She was still bound with seaweed, as she had been when the dolphins captured her, and she looked smaller somehow, as if she had lost something more than just her power. But if anyone had hoped she might show remorse, they were disappointed. Taran was as proud and arrogant as ever. She stared around – and saw Rose.

'*You* –' Her green eyes blazed with fury and she snarled, reminding Lizzy horribly of Tullor. Rose shuddered; Lizzy and Kes put their arms round her shoulders and she turned her head quickly away.

Then Karwynna said, gently but firmly, 'Enough.' She gazed calmly at Taran. 'We're not afraid of you any more, Taran. Your reign is over. Do you have anything to say for yourself?'

Taran glared at the Queen with such hatred that the air seemed to turn cold. 'If you think I'm going to beg forgiveness, you can think again!' she spat. 'I'll die first!'

Karwynna shook her head wearily. 'I have no intention of killing you. That would make me as cruel as you are. I've talked with my people, and we have decided on your punishment. Your servants have deserted you, and if they declare their loyalty to me they will be pardoned. But you will be sent far away, to live out the rest of your life in exile. Dolphins will guard you and make sure that you can't return. You shall never have power again, Taran.'

Taran snarled a second time, but she said nothing. Karwynna sighed, and nodded to the three merpeople.

'Take her to the sea beyond the islands. Our own dolphins will carry her on the first stage of her journey, and others will be waiting to take over from them. She is to go to the other side of the world. And we will be glad to forget her!'

When Taran had been taken away, there was a long silence in the cave before, gradually, like the tide coming in, the talk and laughter began again. Time passed so quickly that Lizzy was startled when Morvyr took her aside and said, 'Lizzy, you must return to land soon, or the potion that Jack and Rose drank will wear off. But before we go Queen Karwynna has something important to ask you.'

'Ask me?' Lizzy's disappointment at the thought of leaving was replaced by curiosity. A little uncertainly she went to sit beside the Queen, who smiled at her.

'Well, Lizzy,' she said. 'The time has come for you to make a decision.'

'A . . . decision, Your Majesty?'

'Yes. You have found your true family, and your true heritage. Will you stay on land − or will you return to your own people?'

'Oh . . .' said Lizzy softly. 'You mean . . . live under the sea, with Kes and Mother?'

Karwynna nodded. 'The choice is yours to make.'

Confused, Lizzy said, 'I − I don't know. I've never thought about it before. I −' She looked in appeal at Jack, who sat nearby. 'What about my father? What's to happen to him?'

'He has already decided. I will remake the boon granted to him by my mother, Queen Kara, so that he can spend time in our world as well as his own. But you are different, Lizzy. You are a true mermaid, and you don't need the magic as Jack does.' She waited. 'What do you think you would like to do?'

And Lizzy realized that she simply didn't know.

'Please, Your Majesty,' she said at last, in a small voice, 'could I have some time to think about it?'

She was afraid that Karwynna might be angry,

but she was not. She laughed, and gave Lizzy a hug. 'Of course you can!' she said. 'Take as long as you wish. But . . .' Her eyes twinkled. 'When you *have* decided, be sure to let us know!'

It was a quieter journey back to St Agnes. Arhans and her friends had stayed behind to join the crowd of seals and dolphins in their celebration, and only Kes and Morvyr swam beside the launch as it motored steadily along. Lizzy and Rose, sitting together behind Jack, were silent. Rose had not overheard Queen Karwynna's talk with Lizzy, but she could guess a lot of it and knew that her sister had a great deal to think about.

At last Rose broke the silence. 'I can still hardly believe all the things that have happened,' she said. 'I mean, I *do*, of course, but . . . mermaids and queens and me going under the sea . . . wow . . . And now it's all over.'

Lizzy looked at her and gave a quick smile. 'No, it isn't,' she said. 'There's still Kes. And Jack. And Morvyr, and Arhans and –'

'OK, OK! Scope for loads more adventures, I know! But they'll be yours, really. Not mine.'

Lizzy didn't answer, and after a minute Rose added, 'We're going home tomorrow.'

'I know.'

'Is that . . . OK?' Rose asked, gently probing. 'I mean . . .' Her voice tailed off.

Lizzy hesitated. Rose clearly had a good idea of what had been said in the rainbow cave and was hoping to learn more. She wanted to give her an answer, but . . .

She stared at the approaching island and said thoughtfully, 'I don't know yet. But maybe if you ask me tomorrow, I will.'

And she gave Rose the biggest and most powerful hug that she could.

Epilogue

The Scillonian ferry turned from the harbourside and slowly gathered speed as she headed out to sea on her journey back to the mainland. Lizzy sat by the stern rail, gazing at the silhouettes of the islands as they grew smaller in the bright afternoon sun. Behind her Mum and Dad had made themselves comfortable; Dad was already dozing and Mum was engrossed in a book. Rose had gone to the onboard shop, and when she came back she joined Lizzy at the rail and pushed a chocolate bar into her hand.

'Your favourite,' she said.

'Oh – thanks.' They unwrapped their bars and

chewed for a minute or two. Then Rose spoke again. 'You said, if I asked you tomorrow. That's today now.'

'Yes. It is, isn't it?' Lizzy scrunched up the chocolate wrapper and put it in her shoulder bag. 'You know what Queen Karwynna asked me, don't you?'

'I think so. About going back to the sea?'

Lizzy nodded. 'I thought about it all last night. And I've decided what to do.'

Rose waited, not daring to ask.

And at last Lizzy said, 'I'm not going back.'

Rose's face lit up like a star. 'Really? Oh, Lizzy! But – are you *sure*?'

Lizzy nodded. 'I was born under the sea, and Morvyr and Jack are my real parents. But I grew up on land. And Mum and Dad . . . they've *always* been Mum and Dad to me, same as to you. And, yes, I found my brother. But I've got a sister too.' For the first time she looked Rose openly in the face. 'I couldn't leave all that, Rose. I just *couldn't*.'

There were tears in her eyes, and Rose felt her own lower lip start to quiver. 'Oh, Lizzy . . .' she said, and held out her arms.

'Don't be a muppet!' Embarrassed, Lizzy pushed her playfully away, then sniffed and wiped her eyes. 'Maybe one day I might go back. But it won't be for years, and I might never do it at all. I mean, I've got the best of both worlds here, haven't I? Kes can come to shore sometimes, and I can visit him and our mother in their world. And Jack'll be here a lot of the time.' She hesitated. 'Besides . . . I *like* growing up on land.'

'Even including school?' Rose asked wickedly.

'Oh, shut up, or I'll change my mind!' Lizzy made a mock swipe at her, then sobered. 'No, seriously, even including school. It's what I *know*, Rose. And I want it to stay that way.'

There was silence for a while. Then Rose said, 'I'm so relieved, sis. I thought . . . well, I thought I was going to lose you. I don't think I can ever tell you how good it is to know that I'm not.'

They were quiet again for a few more seconds. Then:

'You'll have to ask Kes to tea, of course,' Rose said mischievously.

Lizzy giggled as she wondered what Kes would make of human food. She was feeling much better, she realized. Talking to Rose had wiped away the last of her doubts, and she knew for certain now that her decision was right. Morvyr and Kes would understand, she was sure, and so would Queen Karwynna. And maybe, one day in the distant future . . .

'Look!' Rose said softly. 'Dolphins!'

She pointed over the stern. Five dolphins were following them, speeding powerfully and gracefully behind the boat's churning wake. Suddenly, all together, they leaped clear of the water, and as the sunlight caught them Lizzy saw a silver streak down the back of one.

Her heart gave a little skip, and she waved to them. The dolphins plunged back under the surface, and just for a moment Lizzy thought she saw something else. Two shapes . . . the gleam of silvery-green scales . . . dark hair and fair hair, streaming like seaweed as they raced with Arhans and her friends . . .

Happiness washed over her like the rushing current and she blew a kiss that was whisked away on the wind.

'See you soon . . .' she whispered.